Hunks and Horses

Book Two

To Catch A Cowboy

Maggie Carpenter

Published by Dark Secrets Press LLC.

http://www.MaggieCarpenter.com

Cover Image

ROB LANG

https://www.roblangimages.com

Cover Design

FF Designs

Http://fantasiafrogdesigns.wordpress.com

Maggie Carpenter's Books

https://www.Amazon.com/author/maggiecarpenter

CHAPTER ONE

DETERMINATION. THERESA Cavalleri had it in spades, and she was determined to catch herself a cowboy. Not just any cowboy. Josh Brady. Ruggedly handsome, blue-eyed, dark-haired, and sporting a devilish grin, he was a horse trainer at a nearby barn, Tall Tree Farms.

Having recently moved to the country after living in the city since the day she was born, she loved her new life working at Dream Horse Ranch, a sales and training facility. She especially loved the hunky men wearing hats and boots, and when her eyes fell upon Josh, she'd found her man. Not yet brave enough to mount a horse she could only watch as he taught others, and seated in the elevated viewing platform she'd been invisible, then she heard he often spent his evenings at The Horseshoe Tavern.

Dressed in her sexiest jeans and a reddish brown sweater, she headed off to the popular watering hole. Hovering nervously by the door she scanned the room. There was no sign of him. Ambling through the crowd to the bar, she'd just perched on a stool when the swinging doors off to the side caught her attention. A giggling, disheveled blonde appeared, and Theresa guessed the doors led to the rear exit. She grinned knowingly. She'd experienced her share of frantic gropes in back alleys, but her smile quickly faded. Josh emerged.

"What can I get you?"

Jerking her head around, Theresa found a man with twinkling brown eyes staring down at her.

"Do you want a drink?"

"Tequila, a shot."

The bartender turned away, but a split second before he did Theresa noticed his quick scowl in Josh's direction. Shifting on her barstool, wondering why the barman had been irritated, her eyes followed Josh as he sauntered across the room. The blonde peeled off to join a group of girls at a table, and Josh stopped at the vintage juke box.

"Here you go. Tequila shot."

"Thanks," she muttered, swiveling around and pulling her wallet from her bag. "Can you leave the bottle?"

"You can buy a bottle, or I can keep fillin' you up and keep track."

"Yeah. Do that. The filling up," she said, and grabbing the shot she brought it to her lips and threw back her head. "Man! I needed that!" she exclaimed, banging the glass on the counter. "Hit me again."

"You sure you don't wanna pace yourself?"

"Not a chance," she mumbled, looking over her shoulder and seeing a buxom redhead walking up to Josh.

"I haven't seen you in here before," the barman remarked, filling the shot glass.

"That's because this is my first night out since I arrived a few months ago."

"So you're relatively new here."

"Yep," she replied, throwing back the tequila in a single gulp.

"Looks like you've got a taste for that stuff."

"All I've had to drink since I got here is the occasional glass of wine, and I need some Dutch courage tonight."

"The name's Derrick, by the way, but my friends call me Duke."

"Thanks, Duke, I'm Theresa. Theresa Cavalleri."

"Where do you hail from, Theresa?"

"I work at Dream Horse Ranch for Heath and Carly Boyd."

"Small world around here. I'm good friends with them. Are you a new rider?"

"Oh, no. I'm the housekeeper and cook. I want to ride, but I grew up in the city and I'm still nervous around horses."

"Sounds like a story."

"Kinda is," she said, then with a resigned sigh she looked back at Josh. The girl's arm was looped through his. "Shit. I must've been crazy coming here. This is a train wreck."

"How's that?"

"I don't want to look, but I can't help myself," she grumbled, placing her elbow on the counter and dropping her chin in her hand. "This is painful."

"I take it you're interested in Josh Brady."

"I am, but I think I'm wasting my time. Seems he has more women than he can handle. Hard not to want to throw my hat in the ring though."

"Do you like Carrie Underwood?"

"Sure. I didn't listen to country music before I moved here, but now I love it. I prefer the male singers though. Luke Bryan, Blake Shelton, Luke Combs, those guys."

"Have you heard Carrie's song Cowboy Casanova?"

"A few times, but never paid it much attention. Why do you ask?"

"I swear she must have been talkin' about him," Duke said, lowering his voice as he stared across the room at Josh.

"Because?"

"The title says it all."

"Cowboy Casanova? You're saying he's a player?"

"Player? If that means he's like a honey bee buzzin' from flower to flower, yeah, but to be fair I hear he's upfront about things. His line is, I make no promises and I tell no lies."

"Maybe he just hasn't met the right girl."

"Maybe. Give the song a listen next time it comes on. Better yet, mosey on over there and slip a couple of coins in the machine. Here, my treat," he declared, reaching into his pocket and placing two quarters on the counter.

"But he's standing next to it with that hourglass."

"Up to you. Excuse me. I've gotta draw some more beers."

"Pour me another shot first."

"Dang, girl. Let those last two settle for a bit."

"Please, Duke?"

"You've got bigger brown eyes than my horse," he said with a grin.

Reaching for the bottle behind him, he splashed the liquor into her glass, then hurried away. Taking a sip, then another, she moved her eyes back to Josh. The girl whispered in his ear. He shook his head, then landed a smack on her backside.

"Dammit, I wish that was my ass he was slapping," she mumbled under her breath. "Life just isn't fair sometimes."

The coins he'd left seemed to be daring her, and cursing under her breath as she scooped them up, she slid off the stool and moved through the crowd, but as she neared the jukebox she discovered Josh and the redhead had vanished. Simultaneously disappointed and relieved, she dropped the quarters in the slot and selected Cowboy Casanova. Telling herself she wanted some fresh air, but knowing her true motivation was curiosity, she ambled towards the door.

Stepping outside, the cold air pricked her skin. She'd left her leather jacket on the back of the barstool, and crossing her arms she gazed up at the night sky. The rainbow ring around the moon suggested rain. Scanning the parking lot and seeing neither Josh nor the redhead, she was about to head back inside when her eye caught them standing next to a Jeep Cherokee. The redhead had her arms around his neck, and though Josh had his hands on his hips, she'd seen enough. Wishing she was back at the ranch watching television in her cozy cabin, she strode back into the tavern.

He's a good time cowboy Casanova leaning up against the record machine. He looks like a cool drink of water, but he's candy-coated misery.

"Talk about timing," she muttered, making her way to the bar. "This is such bullshit. Of course he's got girls up the wazoo, and even if he didn't, why would he be interested in me? I can't ride, I'm not blonde and perky or red-headed with big boobs. I'm a dark-haired Italian from the streets."

Perching herself on the barstool, she picked up her glass and waved it in the air. Duke, talking to another customer, shot her a wink, then continued his conversation.

"You've got three-seconds to get back here and pour me another drink," she mumbled under her breath, "or I'm out of here."

Though he couldn't have heard, his head abruptly turned in her direction.

Surprised but pleased, she waved the glass a second time.

He held her gaze, but didn't move.

Her stomach did a strange flipping thing.

A wicked grin curling the edges of his lips, he began ambling towards her.

"You got your car keys in that bag of yours?" he asked quietly, resting his hands on the counter, leaning towards her.

"Uh, yeah."

"Let me see them."

Nerves rattling, though not sure why, she reached into her bag and pulled out her key chain, but sensing he planned to snatch them from her hand, she jerked her arm away just as he reached for them.

"I don't think so!" she declared, shooting him a scowl.

"I'm lookin' out for you."

"I can look out for myself!"

"You see anyone in here fallin' down drunk?"

"The night's young. I bet there will be later."

"Probably not. You wanna know why?"

"Not particularly, but I suspect you're going to tell me anyway."

"Two years ago a couple left here and wrapped their car around a tree. Drunk drivin'. That's what did it. They were banged up pretty good, and I thank the Lord every day they weren't killed. That night was a wake-up call. People who come here know they can have a good time, but when I see eyes gettin' bleary and speech gettin' rough, I either cut them off, or they hand in their keys and find another way home. Any bartender who works for me follows that rule."

"Good grief. I've only had three shots, and for the record, I could drink anyone in this place under the table, man or woman. I'm from the streets. I know how to hold my liquor. I also know how to drive buzzed and how to handle myself."

"That right," he drawled, straightening up and crossing his arms.

"Yes, Duke, that's right," she replied, challenge in her eyes. "My glass is empty, and I'm thirsty."

Unmoving, he stared back at her, a glint in his warm brown eyes. A glint she couldn't decipher.

"Please, Duke, Mr. Bartender, person who rules all he surveys," she pleaded, "won't you take pity on a poor girl suffering from unrequited love?"

"You've gotta lotta sass in you, girlie."

"Maybe I do, but I'm still thirsty, and I'll take a beer with that shot," she demanded. As he turned to reach for the bottle, she couldn't see his expression, but she did hear a chuckle. "Mr. Barman, did you hear me?"

"I sure did, Theresa," he replied, moving around and splashing the liquor in her glass.

"Thank you."

"You're welcome, but you might not be thankin' me later."

"Why do you say that?"

"Call it a feelin'," he said with a wink.

CHAPTER TWO

THUNDERING DRUMBEATS rolled through her head. Pain pulsed in her temples. Hearing her own groan, she scrunched her eyes, then slowly opened them. Fuzzy images came into view. A digital clock with glowing blue numbers said 6:47. Time to roll out of bed. She served breakfast at eight o'clock, but as she groggily lifted her head, a slow panic took hold.

She didn't have a bedside clock with blue numbers.

Or a large framed painting hanging on the wall.

Squinting, she tried to bring the image into focus.

A cowboy on a bucking bronco.

"No, no. Please, no. Shit!"

Already aware her whispered plea had been in vain, she shifted slightly and looked over her shoulder. A man apparently in a deep sleep elevated her alarm. Sending her eyes around the foreign bedroom, she spied her jeans, socks and boots on a chair against the wall. Slipping stealthily from the bed, wondering why she was still wearing her Aqua T-shirt, bra and panties, but relieved she was, she crept across the hard-wood floor. Collecting her clothes, she glanced back at the stranger. With only the top of his head showing she had no idea who he was, and she had no desire to wake him to find out. Tiptoeing through the door, closing it softly behind her, she found herself in a hallway.

"I can't believe I did this," she mumbled, pausing to quickly dress. "How the hell am I going to get back to the ranch? Damn, where's my bag?"

A carpet that ran the length of the passage kept her footsteps silent as she walked towards what appeared to be the living room. Her head thumping and feeling nauseous, she barely noticed her surroundings as she searched, though she did spy a cowboy hat sitting on the couch. Finally finding her bag on a table near the front door, stepping outside and meeting the chilly morning air she realized she didn't have her jacket.

"Shit. I must have left it at the Horseshoe," she muttered, toddling forward and staring at the ground as she tried to remember. "How the hell am I going to get home? Salvo! I have to call Salvo."

But as she raised her head to get her bearings, she came to an abrupt halt. Her car was parked at the curb.

"What the hell? I couldn't have driven here. And where the fuck is here? Keys. Where are my keys?"

Setting her bag on the hood, a quick search revealed her keychain in the small zippered pocket. Greatly relieved, she slid behind the wheel, and wanting to put the unfortunate incident behind her, she accelerated to the end of the block without a look back. The late model Land Rover belonged to Dream Horse Ranch, and rolling to a stop, she entered the address into the navigator.

"All because of Josh Fucking Brady," she grunted as the guidance system gave her directions. "Why did I get so plastered?"

Home proved miraculously close, and as Dream Horse Ranch came into view, she pressed the remote control, the gates swung open, and she gratefully turned into the driveway.

She adored her employers, Heath and Carly Boyd. Heath Boyd had rescued her younger brother Salvatore from the inner-city streets, giving him a home and a job at the ranch. It had been several years before that she and Salvatore had been separated under frightening circumstances. After a fruitless search she'd given up hope of ever finding him, but late one night, answering a knock on her door, she'd found him on her porch standing next to a handsome cowboy. She'd been living in a cramped studio apartment, barely making ends meet as a waitress, and Heath Boyd had brought her to the wide open spaces and changed her life. Reunited with her brother, living on the ranch, she had never been happier.

Consumed with guilt, as she passed the main house, she prayed no-one could spot her driving to her cabin, but approaching her carport her heart sank. Salvo was standing by her front door.

"Are you okay?" he demanded as she pulled to a stop and climbed out. "I've been worried sick. Where were you? Why did you stay out all night? I was about to raise the alarm. You didn't answer your phone."

"Calm down. I'm sorry, truly I am."

"You look like shit."

"Thanks."

"What happened," he pressed, following her inside. "Why didn't you call me?"

"Salvo, please stop. I have a raging headache, and I need to take a shower and get changed. Dammit, look at the time."

"Is this about that guy you like? The one at Tall Tree Farms you told me about?"

"Kind of."

"What does that mean?"

"It means I went to The Horseshoe Tavern hoping I'd run into him," she replied, opening a kitchen cabinet and grabbing the aspirin bottle. "I did see him, but it was a disaster. I promise I'll fill in the blanks, at least what I can remember, but right now I have to get my shit together."

"I'm just glad you're okay."

Filling a glass with water, she downed the aspirin, then seeing the angst in her brother's eyes, she set the glass on the counter and walked over to him.

"Hey, I'm a big girl," she said softly, giving him a hug. "I can take care of myself, but I should have called you. I didn't mean to worry you and I'm truly sorry. Am I forgiven?"

"Not yet," he said solemnly, holding her tightly. "You scared me. You really scared me."

Her brother, powerfully built and strong as an ox, suddenly became the frightened child she'd once protected and comforted. Knowing he'd fretted through the night because of her thoughtlessness brought a hot lump to her throat.

"I don't know how, but I'll make this up to you, and I promise I'll never disappear on you again."

Though she needed to hurry, she held him until she heard his telling sigh and he slowly pulled away.

"You'd better get ready," he murmured. "I'll go up and tell everyone you overslept."

"No, Salvo. You mustn't lie for me. Don't volunteer anything, but if someone asks why I'm late, tell them the truth."

"How about we go up to the house together?"

"If you want."

"Yeah. I'd rather wait here while you get ready."

She understood. He needed to stay close. Though he was a strapping young man, the frightened little boy still lived inside him. He didn't realize the ghosts of their past haunted her too.

"No problem. I won't be long."

Entering her bedroom and quickly undressing, she stepped into the shower. As the hot water streamed over her, she closed her eyes, trying to recall the events of the previous evening. There had been dancing and laughing, and Josh had flirted with her.

"Josh!" she exclaimed, opening her eyes and turning off the faucets. "Oh, my God. Did I go home with Josh? No. I'd remember that. The car? How the hell did the car get to that house?"

Though her head was throbbing, her mind continued spinning with questions. Leaving the stall, she hastily dried off, ran a comb through her wet hair, then donned a clean pair of jeans and pink T-shirt.

"Okay, Salvo, let's go," she declared, moving back into the living room.

"But, Theresa, your hair's still wet."

"Can't be helped. I'm actually going to be on time, but I won't be if I pull out my blow dryer."

"Where did you spend the night?" he asked as they climbed into the Land Rover.

"Later, Salvo. Sorry, I didn't mean to snap. I just can't think right now."

"That's okay. I get it."

It was only a thirty-second drive to the main house, and turning into the parking area at the side of the rambling ranch home, she turned off the engine, then leaned back and let out a sigh.

"Thank God. I can't believe I'm not late. You go in the front door like you always do, and I'll go in through the kitchen and get to work."

"Are you sure you're all right?" Salvo asked softly. "Your eyes are bloodshot."

"I'm fine. This isn't my first hangover, but I do have a favor. I think I left my jacket at the tavern."

"Are you talking about Henry?"

"Of course, and I'm worried sick. I'll call over there as soon as—"

"Sis," he said, cutting her off and eyeing her with the hint of a smile, "he's sitting on the back seat."

"What?"

Spinning her head around, then groaning from the effort, she spied the wrinkled, worn, adored leather jacket.

"Thank God!"

"Wow, you must've really been out of it to lose sight of Henry."

"But I don't remember drinking that much and I can hold my liquor."

"Maybe you can't anymore. Maybe you're out of practice."

"You think? I hadn't considered that. You might be right. I haven't had a real drink since I got here."

"I'll bet that's it," Salvo said, sounding wiser than his years. "Your system isn't used to it."

"Damn. That's scary," she muttered as she climbed from the car. "Maybe when we talk later it will help me remember what the hell happened."

Giving him another quick hug, she headed around to the back of the house and walked into the kitchen. A cup of hot sweet tea and a piece of toast would help both her headache and upset stomach. Putting the kettle to boil, she dropped two pieces of bread into the toaster, then moved into the dining room. With Salvo's help the table was set in only a few minutes, and returning to the kitchen she made her tea, buttered her toast, and began to prepare breakfast.

Four others called Dream Horse Ranch home. Heath and Carly lived in the main house. Andy, the barn manager and horse trainer, her brother and her, lived on the property in separate cabins. Though she'd only been there a few months, she couldn't imagine living anywhere else. The open spaces agreed with her, and while the big equines still made her nervous, she held them in awe. Everything about the lifestyle soothed her soul.

"I can't believe I was such an idiot," she mumbled as she cracked eggs into a frying pan. "I need to tell Heath and Carly about last night before they hear what happened from someone else. What a nightmare. All I wanted was for Josh to notice me, but now I'll never be able to face him again. I must have made a total fool of myself."

The sound of voices in the dining room announced the arrival of the small crew. Placing a splatter guard over the top of the pan, she took a breath, then walked through the door.

"Morning, Theresa," Carly said with a smile.

"Morning, Carly. Hi Heath. Is Andy coming?"

"He'll be here shortly."

"The coffee's brewing, but, uh..."

"Theresa, are you okay?" Carly asked. "You look a little pale. Are you coming down with something?"

"The thing is, I went out last night and I'm a bit hungover. Sorry. It won't happen again."

"We all need to blow off steam once and a while," Heath said. "Don't worry about it."

"Thanks. I'll go get that coffee."

Quickly returning to the kitchen, Theresa sank against the door.

"I should have known he'd be nice about it. God, look at me. I'm shaking. Never again. Never, ever again will I do anything to jeopardize my life here."

CHAPTER THREE

DURING THE MORNING meal Carly had remained unusually quiet, and as Andy and Salvo left, Heath put his arm around her shoulders and gave her a squeeze.

"What's on your mind, darlin'?"

"Theresa," she whispered. "I think you should talk to her."

"Hey, that's the first night she's been out since she got here. She's entitled."

"You don't understand. Didn't you see how scared she was when she told us?"

"Can't say's I noticed."

"You're such a guy sometimes."

"I sure hope so."

"She thought you were going to fire her."

"No! Why would she think that?"

"I don't know, and that's my point. She's worried. Go and talk to her. Put her mind at rest."

"You really think I need to?"

"Yes, I do," Carly said solemnly. "We know she and Salvo had things rough, but we don't know how rough. I think Theresa is far more fragile than we know. She puts up a brave front, but she was scared when she came in here. I don't want her to be. I want her to know she's part of the family now. The Dream Horse Ranch family. Please talk to her. I really like her. I want her to feel safe."

"Dang," Heath muttered. "She's always so upbeat and confident."

"I know. It's easy to forget where she came from. Will you talk to her?"

"You bet."

"Thank you," she purred, kissing him on the cheek. "Now I must be off. I need to get down to the barn."

"Please, please watch yourself with Chuck. You know he'll stick his head between his knees and throw you off in a heartbeat."

"Yeah, I know. I'll work him on the ground this morning and see how he is," she said, rising from the table, "but I have to get on him at some point."

"You should let Andy get on him first, and I also think you should wait a couple more days."

"He's already been here a week, and I suspect Chuck would prefer someone light on his back. You take care of Theresa. I'll take care of Chuck."

As Carly headed out, Heath stared at the door that led to the kitchen. Carly had picked up on Theresa's vulnerability. A vulnerability he hadn't noticed.

"I reckon you're right, Carly. I'm a guy, and maybe guys just don't see that stuff."

Pushing back his chair, he ambled across the room, and entering the kitchen he found Theresa loading the dishwasher.

"Hey, when you finish doin' that, why don't you take off and get some rest?"

"I'm okay. The aspirin will kick in soon."

"Theresa, you look knackered. I'm bettin' you didn't sleep so good. You work hard around this place. Take the mornin' off. That's an order."

"Maybe I am a bit under the weather. Thanks, Heath. And I'm sorry. I really didn't mean to get wasted."

"Don't sweat it, and for the record, Carly and I want you to know we're real happy you're here. She's happy to have another woman around the place, and I'm happy because you make the best damn brownies I've ever tasted."

Her brow crinkled, and for a minute Heath thought she was tearing up.

"That's so nice of you," she said softly. "I'm still embarrassed. I honestly don't know what happened last night. I'm sure I didn't drink very much, but I must have. Heath, I, uh...," but her voice trailed off as she lost the courage to tell him about waking up in a stranger's bed.

"You don't have to fill me in on the gory details," he said, sensing the story held more intrigue than knocking back a few drinks. "Like I said before, we all need to blow off a little steam sometimes. Don't give it another thought."

"I didn't go out to blow off steam," she said hastily. "If that had been the plan I wouldn't have taken the Land Rover. I have no reason to blow off steam. I love my job, and I love this ranch. This is the most relaxed I've been in my life."

"If you didn't hit the bars to let loose, do you mind if I ask you why you did?"

"Just one bar. The Horseshoe Tavern, and I went there because I was hoping to run into a cowboy I met. I really like him."

"That's a popular spot. I know the owner, Duke Palmer."

"He mentioned he knew you. He seemed like a nice guy."

"He is. In fact he's bringin' his horse to stay here in the next couple of days. He closes the tavern every couple of months to hunt out new micro-breweries."

"Oh, no. I'll hide. I'm sure I made a fool of myself. I sat at the bar when I first arrived and he took my keys."

"Sounds like him, but you don't have to worry about Duke. I'll bet he's seen a lot worse. So, who is this fella you've got a hankerin' for, if you don't mind me askin'?"

"Josh Brady. He's a trainer over at Tall Tree Farms. Why the frown? Do you know him?"

"Met him once. I can understand why you like him. He's a good-lookin' guy."

"And funny. He has everyone in stitches during his lessons. Unfortunately he doesn't even know I'm alive."

"Maybe that's just as well," Heath remarked. "A package can be wrapped up pretty, but there's no tellin' what you might find when you open it up."

"I take it you don't like him."

"He hasn't been in this area very long, but he's already gettin' quite the reputation."

"Do you think he's bad news?"

"Let's just say I've heard stories."

"He is a flirt, that's for sure."

"Did you spend any time with him?"

"I remember dancing with him, but most of the evening is a blur. Not that it matters. I doubt he has any interest in me," she said with a heavy sigh. "I'd really like to meet someone, and Josh is the first guy I've come across I really like."

"Uh-huh. Well, Theresa, it's your life and your heart, but I'd steer clear. Why don't you finish up and go on back to your cabin for a nap."

"I still feel guilty. I shouldn't let my personal life get in the way of my job."

"What personal life? One night and a little too much to drink? You're makin' too much of this. Don't give it a second thought."

"Thanks so much, Heath. I really appreciate you taking the time to come in here and talk to me. I know how busy you are."

"People come first. You take it easy, and don't come back until you're feelin' better."

She waited until he left, then sank into a chair at the kitchen table. Her headache pounding through her temples, she dropped her head in her hands.

"This is seriously depressing. I find a guy I'm totally into, and it turns out he's probably an asshole. Is there such a thing as a cowboy who's an asshole? That's depressing by itself. Heath's right about one thing. I need to lie down."

Slowly getting to her feet, she finished loading the dishwasher, then stepped outside and climbed into the Land Rover. It was hers to use as she needed, but she only left the ranch to do errands and visit Tall Tree Farms. Her excursion to The Horseshoe Tavern had been the first time she'd ventured out after dinner.

"I won't be doing that again in a hurry," she muttered as she drove down to her cabin. "Dammit, I need to get to the store. I'd better make a list. I don't trust myself to remember anything today."

Rolling under the carport, she climbed out, grabbed her much-loved, battered leather jacket from the back seat, walked into the quaint cottage and straight to the bedroom. Kicking off her shoes, she collapsed on the bed, and letting out a groan, she closed her eyes and prayed for sleep.

She was standing in the middle of a paddock. Stars twinkled overhead, the air was crisp, and the spooky hoot of an owl echoed through the dark. A sound made her turn. Walking toward her, Josh's dimpled grin sent a flurry of excitement through her belly. The cool breeze sent her nipples puckering under her thin T-shirt, and his gaze dropped to stare at them. Unable to hide her aching desire, she knew his slow amble was designed to tease.

"Hey, girl. Whatta you doin' out here in the middle of the night?"

"Waiting for you," she replied, her breathless whisper all she could manage.

"What do I have that you want?"

"I saw you spank that girl at the tavern."

"And?"

"And I want you to spank me. The thought of it makes me crazy. I love to be spanked."

She paused, though she didn't know why. He was so handsome, and she'd been waiting for this moment for weeks.

Thundering hooves shattered the silence. Darting her eyes to the fields behind the arena, a huge chestnut horse with a roached flaxen mane and white blaze galloped towards them. The magnificent creature leapt over the fence, clearing it with air to spare. Though her heart raced, she felt no fear, and turning to face the noble animal, a sense of deep calm filled her soul. Breaking to a trot as it neared, the horse stopped beside her and lowered its head.

"See that?" Josh said as she stroked the horse's neck. "You don't have to be afraid. Not of anything."

Her eyes popped open.

She was hugging her extra pillow.

Her headache had receded to a shadowy ache.

Rolling on her back, she stared at the ceiling.

"Josh Brady, maybe you're not a bad guy after all, but it wasn't you in that bed this morning. I don't know why I know that, but I do."

Sitting up, she glanced at the clock on the wall. Set in a hand-carved wooden barn, a horse sat on the end of the minute hand, forever circling the numbers. She'd been sleeping for almost three hours. Feeling well enough to return to work and prepare lunch, she slipped from her bed, washed her face, brushed her hair, and changed out of her wrinkled shirt.

Stepping outside, a cool breeze touched her face, but as she opened the door to climb into the Land Rover, she paused. The house sat up the driveway to her right, but to her left were the grassy paddocks where the horses spent their days. Impulsively she turned and strode towards them.

Though she loved watching the animals frolic, she lacked confidence when she drew close. They were big, and their long teeth and powerful jaws could bite off a finger. Carly had shown her how to rest a treat in the palm of her hand and bend back her fingers, but she didn't have the nerve to hold her hand still when the horse leaned down to gobble it up.

Reaching the first pasture, the two horses raised their heads, pricked their ears, and strolled towards the fence. They knew a visitor meant carrots! Feeling guilty for arriving empty-handed, Theresa jogged into the nearby barn and grabbed a handful from the feed room. By the time she returned, all the horses were at the railing waiting. She laughed out loud.

"You guys are so adorable. I won't be able to hand-feed you, but I'll toss your treats into the field," she promised as she walked quickly forward.

Exiting the outdoor ring on her way to the barn, Carly was leading a large-boned, roan quarter horse named Chuck. Surprised to see Theresa at the pasture, she veered off the path to join her.

"Theresa! Hi," she called as she moved down the gentle bank. "I take it you're feeling better."

"Hi, Carly. I am, thank you, and I had the most amazing dream about a horse. When I woke up my headache was gone and I wanted to pay these guys a visit."

"That's great on both counts."

"I don't know if I'll ever be able to ride, but just being around them is wonderful. They're so beautiful."

"Yes, they are. They're individuals with likes and dislikes, and their own personalities, but if they trust you they reveal themselves."

"How do you get them to do that?"

"Learn how to listen. Take this guy for example," she remarked, sliding her hand along his neck. "If I try to scratch his ears, watch what happens."

Carly raised her hand, but before she could touch him, he ducked his head away.

"Why did he do that?"

"Could be anything. People sometimes twist a horse's ear to keep them still for various reasons, or he might have an infection. The vet will be here soon to give him the once over, and if there's no physical reason for the reaction, it means this poor guy has had bad handlers, but Theresa, I think your new friends want those carrots you're holding."

Turning around, the horses stared at her, silently begging her to feed them, some tossing their heads impatiently.

"I didn't mean to torture you," she said with a giggle. "I'm coming, but you look too hungry to risk my fingers. I'll see you up at the house, Carly. I thought I'd make tuna salad for lunch."

"That's sounds great. I'm glad you're feeling better."

"Thanks. Me too."

As Carly started toward the barn, Theresa walked hesitantly up to the fence line, tossed the carrots into the field, and watched the grateful horses chase after them. There were four paddocks, and when she reached the last one she was tempted to step closer and offer the treat by hand. To her dismay, she lost the nerve.

"I'll get there," she promised herself as she threw the last few into the paddock. "I don't know how, but I will."

Though smiling as she headed back to her cabin and the Land Rover, her mind turned from her pleasant interlude with the horses, to her unsettling morning.

"I wish I'd taken note of the address of that house. The navigator! Of course. The navigator will take me back there, but do I want to go? I sure as hell want to know who he was, but I don't want him to see me. I need to think about this. I'll talk to Salvo. Maybe between the two of us we can come up with a plan."

CHAPTER FOUR

LUNCH HAD BEEN SERVED, everyone had left the house, and sitting at the kitchen table Theresa was writing out her shopping list. Though her headache had passed, a vague weariness lingered and she found it difficult to concentrate. Stifling a yawn, she thought about brewing a fresh pot of coffee, but decided instead to drop into the local cafe. Run by Andy's girlfriend Maureen O'Toole, the coffee shop offered delicious cakes, cookies and pies. Taking five minutes to enjoy someone else's baking was decidedly appealing. Adding the last few items to the list, she was rising from the table when Carly walked in. Theresa knew immediately something was wrong.

"Carly? Are you okay?"

"I think so," she mumbled dropping into a chair. "Do we have any lemonade?"

"Sure. I made a fresh batch yesterday," Theresa replied, fetching a glass from the cupboard. "What happened?"

"I got dumped," Carly groaned as Theresa placed the drink in front of her. "Chuck bucked me off. I can't believe it. I was totally prepared and he still got the better of me."

"No! Oh, my gosh. How? Why? Are you all right?"

"I haven't hit the dirt in ages. He threw me a crazy buck out of nowhere. That's why he's called Chuck. He's famous for chucking people off his back. I don't know what's wrong with him. The vet came and went, said he was fine. I got on, and a minute later I was on the ground. I don't get it."

"That is so scary," Theresa muttered as she sat down. "Where is he now?"

"Andy untacked him and put him in a paddock. But I don't want to hold you up. I know you need to get to the store."

"Is there anything I can do for you before I go?"

"She's gettin' straight into a hot bath with Epsom Salts," Heath declared, marching into the kitchen. "The tub's already fillin' up. I've been lookin' for you, Carly. Andy texted me. Dang, girl. Are you okay?"

"Just embarrassed, and I needed a drink," Carly said, then finishing the last of her lemonade, she rose slowly to her feet.

"I had a bad feelin' about you gettin' on him," Heath remarked. "I know you're a great rider, but I don't want you gettin' on him again."

"He seemed fine," Carly said with a weary sigh, leaning against him. "I'll figure it out. I just need some more time with him."

"On the ground. I mean it, Carly. You're not ridin' him again. Come on, let's get you into that hot water."

"Uh, Heath, I'm going into town," Theresa said, admiring how Heath was so protective of the woman he loved. "Do you need anything?"

"Can't think of anything, Theresa, but thanks. Drive safe. One casualty is already one too many."

"Feel better, Carly."

"Thanks. I'll be sore for a couple of days, but I didn't break anything, thank God. I'll see you later."

"Riding is dangerous, too dangerous for me," she said under her breath, as Carly limped away.

Picking up her shopping list, she stuffed it into her purse and headed out the back door. Climbing into the Land Rover, she headed into town listening to the country and western radio station, singing along with her favorite tunes. When Cowboy Casanova came on, she flashed back to the previous night.

"Maybe he's getting a reputation because he's so cute. I can see why he'd be a heartbreaker, but it's not his fault if the girls fall for him. Duke said he makes no promises. Shit. Duke. I can't believe he's coming to the ranch. I wonder if I was with him last night? Oh, dear God, I hope not. Why is everything a mess all of a sudden?"

Out of sorts, she pulled into the grocery store parking lot, rolled to a stop, and grabbing her purse she climbed from the car.

"I'm so not in the mood for this," she mumbled, entering the store. "I can't wait for that cup of coffee at Maureen's."

Taking her time, she picked up the many things she needed, and by the time she approached the cashier's line there was no room left in her cart. Finally checked out, she pushed the heavy load outside, but as she started across the parking area a familiar voice called her name.

Josh Brady.

Her heart skipped a beat.

"Let me help you."

Turning around, the smiling, handsome cowboy strode towards her.

"How many mouths do you have to feed," he joked as he reached her.

"Uh, four, no, five, including me," she replied nervously, thinking he looked cuter than ever. "I'm the cook at Dream Horse Ranch, or do you know that already?"

"Nope. You didn't mention that last night. I hear it's quite a spread," he said, taking control of the cart and moving it forward. "Where's your car?"

"The white Land Rover over there, and yes, it's a beautiful property."

"Where is it exactly?"

"At the end of Bluebell Lane."

"Great spot," he remarked, stopping at the car.

Theresa unlocked the tail gate, and together they unloaded the bags from the trolley.

"Thanks so much, Josh."

"Are you in a hurry?"

"Uh, no. I was planning a cup of coffee at Maureen's cafe."

"Mind if I join you? I wanted to spend more time with you last night, but I never got the chance."

Theresa's face flushed red, but she had no idea how to respond.

"But hey, here we are," Josh exclaimed, quickly easing the awkward moment. "Now we'll be able to have a proper conversation. I'd like to know more about you. Let's go. Have you ever had Maureen's banana cream pie?"

"I haven't," she replied as they started off. "I usually have the fruit tart or a blueberry muffin."

"You're in for a treat, but there's a condition."

"A condition? How can there be a condition to eating banana cream pie?"

"You'll find out," he quipped, shooting her a wink, "and I want an answer to the question I asked you last night."

"What question is that?"

"Why do you sit and watch? Why don't you ever take a lesson?"

"I'm not ready," she said, willing her heart to stop hammering and her butterflies to stop fluttering. "I love horses, but they scare me, and I'm afraid I'll fall off. Even good riders hit the ground, so I'm bound to."

"Hey, the good riders fall off more than beginners. They take more chances. I take it you're not from around here."

"No, I grew up in the city. This is all new to me, but I love it. I love everything about it."

They'd reached the coffee shop, and holding the door open, he ushered her inside.

"What would you like?" he asked as she walked past him.

"A Grande Latte, please."

"Grab us a table. I'll be right there."

"Thank you."

"My pleasure."

Choosing a spot near the window, she sat down and watched him pick up two coffee mugs and head towards her. He carried himself with an easy gait, and when he reached her, his blue eyes twinkled down at her as he placed their drinks on the table.

"She's bringin' the pie."

"Great, thanks, Josh."

"Tell me, Theresa, what's it gonna take for me to get you into a saddle."

"Several shots of whiskey," she said with a giggle.

"Yeah, well, that's not gonna happen, not on my watch."

"I was kidding, but only partly. I have the desire, but not the nerve."

"The next time you're at Tall Tree, you're gettin' on board."

"Holy crap. You may never see me again."

"That would be a crime, and I'm no lawbreaker."

"Here's your pie," Maureen declared, setting the scrumptious-looking desert on the table. "I brought two spoons. I figured you'd want to share it. Hello, Theresa."

"Hi, Maureen. Thank you. That looks delicious."

"I like to think it is."

As she walked way, Theresa reached for a spoon, but Josh snatched it away.

"That condition I mentioned," he said, lowering his voice and leaning over the table.

"Okay," Carly said warily. "I'm listening."

Wordlessly Josh scooped up a spoonful of the rich dessert, and held it to her lips.

"I get to feed it to you."

"Josh Brady. You are such a flirt."

"Uh-huh. Open wide."

"And if I refuse?"

"But you won't."

"How can you be so sure?"

"Two reasons. The first, I'm bettin' you love banana cream pie."

"And the second."

"The second I'm keepin' for another time. Now be good and open wide."

He was weaving his spell, and even though she knew it, she was unable to resist. As Josh placed the creamy sweet in her mouth, she rolled her eyes and softly moaned.

"That is divine."

"Uh-huh."

"And you are incorrigible. In fact, that's how I'll refer to you from now on. The Incorrigible Cowboy."

"I like it," he said with a chuckle, taking a bite of the pie for himself.

They fell into an easy camaraderie as he continued to feed her the rich dessert, the time flying by as they laughed and chatted about horses. When Theresa finally checked her watch, she was shocked to see almost an hour had passed.

"I can't believe it. Thank you, Josh. I've had a really nice time, but I need to get back to the ranch."

"Hey, it's been great, and I'm glad I got the chance to spend some time with you before I take off."

"Take off?" she repeated, feeling her heart sink. "Where are you going?"

"There's a four-week show up in Springdale leadin' into the regional championships."

"Where's Springdale? The name rings a vague bell, but I haven't been out exploring very much."

"Only about an hour away. We're headin' out tomorrow, but I'm not sure how long we'll be gone."

"Why is that?"

"Depends on how well we're doin', but when I get back, you're climbin' into that saddle."

"Oh, my gosh."

"I've gotta feelin' once you're up there I'll have a hard time gettin' you out."

"You might be right about that," she said with a giggle. "I do love the thought of it."

"How would you like to do me a favor?"

"If I can."

"I'm not competin', just trainin', so my own horse isn't comin'. She's a real sweetheart, and I know she'll be fed and taken out to her pasture every day, but maybe you could swing by when you have a minute and give her some attention."

"I, uh, I'd like to, but I don't know what I could do."

"Just stand by the fence and talk to her. She'll come up and visit with you. If you're nervous about feedin' her carrots, you can toss them on the ground, but you don't have to be. She's a lamb. I'd sure appreciate it, Theresa. She's a special girl and she's used to that kind of attention."

"I'd love to visit her. What's her name?"

"Queenie."

"Queenie? That's adorable."

"She's royalty as far as I'm concerned. Do you think you can get away late tomorrow mornin'?"

"That won't be a problem. What did you have in mind?"

"Come over to Tall Tree and I'll introduce you to her before I leave. We'll be takin' off around noontime."

"I need to have lunch ready by then. I can come over around ten-thirty if that's okay."

"Sounds good to me. Let's exchange numbers in case something comes up, and while I'm gone you can call if you have any questions. I'd like to check in anyway."

"Sure," she said, grabbing her bag and retrieving her phone. "I'll text it to you. What's yours?"

"Here's my card," he said, pulling out his wallet and handing it to her. "I've gotta keep tabs on you. I need to know if you'll need a spankin' when I get back."

"Excuse me?" she stammered, staring at him wide-eyed.

"Don't look so shocked. You begged me for one last night."

"I did not!"

"Uh, yeah, you did, Princess," he said, lowering his voice, "and I promised I'd deliver, but I didn't get the chance."

"I am so embarrassed right now. Much of last night is a blur."

"You were pretty wasted."

"Just one thing, Josh. A birdie told me you don't make promises."

"I don't make promises I'm not sure I can keep, but that one was a no-brainer, and it's still good. Just remember, you opened the door."

"Good grief. I didn't expect a conversation like this when I agreed to have a cup of coffee with you."

"You know what they say. Life is full of surprises."

"Can we please change the subject?"

"You bet, but I know you have to go, and I need to get back to the barn," he said, grinning his wicked grin. "I only stopped at the store to pick up some snacks for the trip. I'm glad I did."

"Me too. Thanks for the coffee and pie."

"My pleasure. And I mean that."

Titillated by the tantalizing conversation, they left the table and started to the door, but as they stepped outside, he took her hand. Her heart skipped, and she decided the stories Heath had heard about Josh were just that, stories. Behind the handsome face and naughty flirty, she sensed a kind, decent man.

Both parked in the supermarket lot, they strolled across to the store. His fingers held hers tightly, and she squeezed his in response. Her body and heart responded, and when they reached the Land Rover she put up no resistance when he pulled her into his arms. He held her for a moment, then his hand slid into her hair and tugged back her head. Closing her eyes and holding her breath, she waited to feel his mouth on hers. Initially it was a soft touching of lips, then his tongue slid between her teeth as he pressed harder. Circling his neck with her arms, she fervently kissed him back. The timeless liplock sent waves of need through her being, and finally breaking apart she melted against him, praying the moment would never end.

The chestnut horse with the roached mane unexpectedly galloped through her mind's eye, and the words Josh had spoken in the dream echoed through her head.

You don't have to be afraid. Not of anything.

CHAPTER FIVE

LEANING AGAINST JOSH'S chest and wrapped in his muscled arms had been sheer heaven—and his kiss. His kiss had been sublime, and his hardness pressed against her thigh made her wish he would scoop her up and carry her away in his truck. The radio blasting her favorite tunes, when Luke Bryan began singing Most People Are Good, she took it as a sign.

"Yes, they are," she exclaimed, "and that includes Josh Brady."

Arriving at the ranch—her hangover a distant memory—she unloaded the groceries, then decided to cook up one of her favorite dishes for the evening meal; chicken and dumplings.

Carly had spent the day resting in her room, but reappeared for dinner. Heath and Andy wanted to talk to her about Chuck, and dissect exactly what had happened before the horse had thrown her off his back. The cause of the ongoing issue was baffling. Only ten years old, the gelding had been a star, then out-of-nowhere began bucking. A small fortune had been spent attempting to diagnose the problem, but with no answers the owners called Heath asking if he'd like to take the former champion off their hands. Carly and Andy were familiar with the roan gelding, and believed him to be worth effort. As they ate the meal and discussed various theories, Theresa sat quietly daydreaming about Josh.

The first couple of weeks at Dream Horse Ranch she'd wandered around in a daze. The closest she'd ever been to the open spaces was the city park, and though the quiet evenings took some getting used to, she'd never slept better, and the permanent tension living in her shoulders slowly dissolved.

And then there were the cowboys.

31

There was something about boots and cowboy hats she found irresistible. When she accepted Heath's offer to replace the outgoing house manager, though she knew the title was a fancy name for cook/housekeeper, she was thrilled, but if she was going to stay she wanted a man with boots and a hat to call her own. With Carly's encouragement she'd set about catching herself a cowboy. Now she dared to hope the mission had been successful. A smart, savvy city girl, she knew Josh's favor—visiting his mare—gave him the excuse to stay in touch with her. She smiled a secret smile, and glancing at Heath she sent him a silent message.

You might know about horses, but you're wrong about Josh. Those rumors you heard are bullshit.

"Man that was good," Andy declared, setting down his knife and fork. "Thanks, Theresa."

Startled by her name, she snapped her head around and blinked at him.

"The chicken and dumplin's. Great."

"I'm glad you enjoyed it," she replied, quickly gathering her wits. "I hope you have room left for peach cobbler."

"I'd love to have some, but I promised Maureen I'd head over to her place. She wanted me there for dinner, but I couldn't make it so we settled on sharing apple pie."

"Then you'd better not keep her waiting."

Worried Maureen might mention seeing her with Josh, then Andy might say something to Heath, Theresa frantically searched for a tactful way of getting ahead of the story by broaching the subject.

"Feel better, Carly," Andy said, rising to his feet. "I'll give Chuck another goin' over tomorrow."

"I can't imagine what it could be," Carly said wearily. "The chiropractor and vet checked him out, and the Wilsons ran all those tests."

"You and I both know horses don't act like that unless there's a reason. We've just gotta find out what that is. I'll see you tomorrow."

Theresa silently groaned. The opportunity to speak up about being at Maureen's cafe with Josh had passed, but as she cleared the table and carried the plates into the kitchen, she decided her personal life was no-one else's business. Heath had said so himself.

Theresa, it's your life and your heart.

"Yes it is," she muttered, placing the dishes in the sink and turning her attention to spooning out the cobbler. "I'm not an idiot. Josh is single and he's sexy as hell. I see the girls at the barn throw themselves at him, and if he's upfront about things, then there's no harm, no foul."

"Hey, sis. What are you mumbling about?"

Looking up, her brother ambled towards her.

"Hi. I didn't see you there. Do you need something?"

"Nope. I'm here to help you carry in the dessert plates."

"Thanks, that's sweet of you. Be a doll and grab the ice cream from the freezer?"

"Can I come back to your cabin with you?" he asked, fetching the frozen container and placing it on the counter.

"Sure, but not for too long. I need an early night."

"I bet you do."

"Is that why you want a chat?" she inquired, giving him a look as she scooped out the ice cream.

"Hell, yeah. I want to know what happened. I've been thinking about it all day. I'm worried."

"Why? I'm here, safe and sound."

"I'll tell you later. Are these ready?"

"Yep. I'm right behind you."

Picking up two of the dishes with the dollops of ice cream, Salvo carried them into the dining room, and after putting away the container, Theresa quickly followed. She could understand her brother's concern. Her blackout bothered her as well.

"Thanks, Theresa. This looks great," Heath declared as she returned and sat down. "I forgot to mention, Duke Palmer called. He's bringing his horse in tomorrow morning."

"Off on one of his beer hunting quest, I assume," Carly remarked. "I don't know how he can afford to close up like he does."

"He makes a mint in that place, and he hasn't been on one of his excursions for a few months. He mentioned he'd like to say hello to you, Theresa. Will you be around?"

"What time is he coming?"

"He didn't say exactly, but I expect it'll be mid-morning."

"I'm not sure I'll be here," Theresa replied, praying she'd be gone when he showed up. "I have an errand to run."

"Heath, my back's bothering me," Carly mumbled. "I need to get out of this chair."

"I'll get you an ice bag," Theresa offered, jumping from her seat and moving quickly into the kitchen.

"Carly, you must get checked out tomorrow," Heath said softly. "At the very least the doc can give you an anti-inflammatory and something more than aspirin for the pain."

"I'll be fine. Besides, the thought of getting into a car sounds dreadful."

"Then I'll call Dr. Briggs and have him come here, and I'm not debating this. If he says you need X-rays, then—"

"Then we can have the vet come back and use his mobile unit."

"Fair enough."

"I'll go and check on that ice for you," Salvo said, rising to his feet. "I'm sorry you're hurting, Carly. I wish there was something I could do."

"I'm okay. Just banged up a bit."

Moving through the door and entering the kitchen, Salvo found Theresa standing next to the refrigerator, the chilled pack in her hands.

"What are you doing?"

"I don't want to get cornered about seeing Duke Palmer tomorrow," she said hastily. "I think Heath is trying to play matchmaker, and I have zero interest in that guy. Here. Take this in for me."

"Sure," Salvo said, accepting the ice pack, "but I think Heath was just making conversation."

"I don't want to take that chance."

"Whatever," Salvo muttered, shrugging his shoulders.

As he carried it away, Theresa poured herself a cup of coffee and dropped into a chair. Things were getting complicated, but as she thought about Josh, and how she'd felt being wrapped up in his arms, her stomach flipped.

"I can't wait to see you, Josh Brady. I absolutely cannot wait."

"They've left," Salvo declared, breaking into her reverie as he walked in carrying the dessert dishes. "Can we get things cleared up and go? I really want to talk to you."

"Sounds good to me. I want to talk to you too. Is that rain I hear?"

"I think it is. Was rain in the forecast? I missed the weather."

"I'll check my phone."

Pulling it from her bag, she was about to hit the weather app when a notification told her she had a text from Josh. Breaking into a happy grin, she tapped the screen.

Hey Princess.

The banana cream pie was delicious, but not half as delicious as you. See you tomorrow around 10:30.

Josh. OX's

"Good news, huh?" Salvo guessed, studying her expression.

"What? Uh, in a way." Lifting her eyes, his burning curiosity burned across at her. "I'll explain when we're in my cabin."

"What about the weather?"

"Oh, right. Hang on. I need to reply to this first."

Hello Josh.

The coffee was great, but the dessert was amazing, and I'm not talking about the banana cream pie.

Princess. OX's

"The weather?" Salvo pressed.

"I'm getting it," Theresa said impatiently, wondering if she should have signed off, *Princess.* "Oh, wow. Thunderstorms overnight, then clearing with a chance of showers tomorrow. I didn't hear anything about thunderstorms."

"Seasons are changing. Things can get hairy around here in a heartbeat. I told you what happened when Carly first arrived. She was almost killed in a storm."

"Of course I remember that story," Theresa said, putting her phone away and starting on the dishes.

"Just be careful if you're out and unexpected weather hits. Don't try driving back. Call and let me know where you are, and stay put."

"Seriously?"

"Yeah, seriously."

"Huh. Okay. If you clear the table, I'll stack the dishwasher."

"Deal."

Working as a team they quickly finished, then hurried out the back door and into the Land Rover. Driving slowly through the downpour, a flash of lightning lit up the sky as she pulled under the carport.

"I almost wish I was back in the house."

"Except the house is on the top of the knoll. We have more protection."

"Do the horses get worked up in weather like this?" she asked as they walked quickly inside. "Do you need to check on them? Andy's not here and Carly's laid up."

"They're usually fine, but I'll swing by the barn when I leave. Heath will probably come down at some point. He usually does in bad weather even if Andy is around."

"Can I get you anything? I'm going to have a glass of wine."

"No thanks," Salvo said, perching on one of the bar stools in front of the kitchen counter. "Just tell me about last night. You went to The Horseshoe Tavern hoping to run into Josh Brady. Was he there?"

"He was definitely there," Theresa replied, pouring herself a glass of white wine, "but I need to start with Duke Palmer, the bartender, and I guess he's also the owner."

"The guy bringing in the horse tomorrow."

"Exactly. I got the feeling he liked me, even though he didn't make it obvious. When I first arrived, Josh came in from the back exit with a blonde, and the next minute some redhead was all over him. Duke compared him to that song, Cowboy Casanova. I remember going to the jukebox, but Josh had disappeared with that redhead so I checked the parking lot and saw him with her at his truck. I went inside, and except for a vague recollection of dancing with Josh at some point, everything's a blank. How can that be?"

"But where did you spend the night?"

"Salvo, this part is bizarre. I woke up in a guy's bed, but I don't think anything happened. I was still in my underwear and T-shirt. I have no idea how I got there, and when I snuck outside the Land Rover was parked at the curb."

"That is really weird, but Theresa, there's a part of your story that rings a bell. Remember that night you went to a club and a guy slipped you a roofie? Your girlfriends got you out of there and you didn't recall much of anything the next day. You had a killer headache as well."

"Oh, my gosh, you're right. Holy crap!"

"The only thing is, if the guy you woke up with had done that, I think—"

"I would have woken up naked," she said, interrupting him. "Shit. Do you think a Knight in Shining Armor rescued me?"

"Can you think of anything else that makes sense? You slipped away before he could tell you, or he figured you'd be embarrassed and pretended to be asleep so you could sneak out."

"I wonder who it was."

"Before we get in to that, did any other guy hit on you? What about when you were sitting at the bar? Do you remember anyone next to you?"

"Salvo, the place was jammed. Anyone could have dropped something in my drink."

"Where is this house? Do you know how to get there?"

"I used the navigator to find my way home, so yeah, I can find it again. I just don't know if I want to."

"I'll drive over there tomorrow night and stake it out, assuming we're not in the middle of a storm."

"We should do it together, but there's more."

"Damn, Theresa. More?"

"Yeah. I ran into Josh at the supermarket today. We shared a cup of coffee and I had the best time. I like him so much. He's asked me to visit his mare while he's away at a horse show. I'm going to see him tomorrow after breakfast."

"Oh, no. I can see it written all over your face. You're toast."

"I'm sure Heath and Duke are wrong about him. He might get around, but he's a good-looking guy and he's single. Why shouldn't he? There's no law against a guy having a good time."

"Sounds like you're making excuses for him," Salvo said solemnly.

"I'm just stating the obvious."

"Don't jump into anything."

"Too late. After today I'm already in. Andy's with Maureen right now, and earlier I was worried she might say something about seeing us together, then Andy would tell Heath, and I know Heath doesn't like Josh Brady, but—"

"Stop!"

"Why?"

"You need to listen to me. Heath is the best thing that's happened to us. He rescued me from the streets, then brought me here and gave me a life. He's the reason we found each other, and he took you out of that hovel and that awful waitressing job."

"I am very aware of all that, and I'll be eternally grateful to him, but remember what mom used to say about that awful man who called himself our father? You can't help who you fall in love with."

"I haven't finished," Salvo said, his voice suddenly sounding older than his years. "Heath or no Heath, at the end of the day you have to live and die by your choices. You can seek advice, but the decisions you make are yours to bear, whether they lead to triumph or tragedy. Don't let anyone stop you from doing what you want, or push you into doing something you feel is wrong."

Theresa sat silently staring at her little brother, then putting down her wine glass, she stepped around the kitchen counter and hugged him.

"How did you get so smart? Thank you."

"Being around guys like Heath and Andy, stuff like that kind of rubs off. Anything else?"

"No. I think I'll watch some TV then go to bed."

"I'm off to the barn, then I'll be hitting the sack as well. Can I give you another piece of advice?"

"Absolutely."

"This guy, he's used to girls chasing him. Be different."

"I'm not a game player."

"No, and I'm not suggesting that, but I am suggesting you value your worth, and make sure he does too."

CHAPTER SIX

IN SPITE OF THE OVERNIGHT storm Theresa woke from a glorious sleep. Delightful dreams of the beautiful chestnut with the white blaze and roached mane had given way to salacious scenes starring her handsome cowboy. The steed had sprouted mighty wings, and sitting astride with no saddle or bridle, Theresa had flown to a magic meadow where Josh waited with open arms.

A white fluffy blanket sat on the lush green grass near a gentle waterfall with a rainbow halo splashing into a crystal clear pond. Laying her down, he lovingly kissed her naked skin as he slowly peeled off her clothes, then spanking her with sweet, stinging slaps, set about devouring her body with heart-stopping passion.

Though still groggy, the urgent need between her legs sent her fingers to her clit, and as she fervently rubbed, fresh fantasies took hold. Josh pinned her wrists as he breathed wicked promises in her ear, then moving his mouth to her breasts, he drew in her nipples and sucked hungrily before flipping her over. His hot hand smacked her backside, and only when she begged for his cock did he thrust inside her and pummel her pussy with powerful strokes.

The orgasm fired.

Tingling pins and needles rippled through her limbs.

Wave after wave of sizzling sensations swept her away.

Serenity settled.

She drifted, then slowly opened her eyes.

"I must have you, Josh Brady. I must and I will."

The whispered promise still on her lips, she glanced at the clock on her wall, smiling as she watched the horse on its infinite journey ticking in a circle. Seven-thirty. Time to get out of bed, drive up to the house and get breakfast on the table. Stretching her arms above her head, she let out a long yawn, followed by a happy sigh, then slipping from the bed, she ambled to the window and stared out at the day. The wet ground, evidence of the night's tempest, sparkled in the morning sun, and puffy clouds traversed the sky.

Showering and quickly dressing, she grabbed her favorite leather jacket, named Henry after the biker who had so generously given it to her one cold winter night, and wrapping a white wool scarf around her neck, she climbed in the Rover and headed up to the house. The day was nippy and filled with promise. She would soon be driving to Tall Tree Farms.

But the morning proved to be a busy one. Busier than she'd anticipated.

After serving a breakfast of ginger fruit compote and black walnut pancakes, she set about preparing a cob salad for lunch. Serving the mid-day meal at noon meant she'd have to be back in the kitchen by eleven-thirty at the latest, but if she had everything ready, she could push that back if things with Josh were going well. As she daydreamed about him while dicing vegetables, the phone rang startling her, and the sharp paring knife slipped. The cut on her forefinger spouted blood, and hurriedly wrapping a paper towel around the gushing wound, she grabbed the receiver.

"Hello?"

"Hi. Is this Theresa?"

"Yes. Can I help you?"

"This is Duke Palmer. Remember me? I own The Horseshoe Tavern."

"Of course. Hi, Duke."

"I'm at the gate. Can you buzz me in?"

"Sure," she replied, pressing nine on the phone's keypad wishing someone else had picked up the phone.

But there was no-one else.

In spite of Heath's protests, Carly had insisted she be present while Andy gave Chuck another examination. Heath wasn't about to leave her side, and though Dr. Briggs was due any time, Heath drove her down in the ATV. Though Theresa didn't understand why Carly would leave the comfort of her bed while in pain, or why Heath would comply, she had more important things on her mind, and making sure she wasn't held up sat at the top of the list.

Hastily removing the blood-soaked paper, she replaced it with another, and managed to don a rubber glove to keep the makeshift dressing in place. The sound of a truck and horse trailer told her Duke was passing the house. She thought about calling Heath to alert him, then immediately dismissed the idea.

"I am not going to get stuck here playing host to you, Duke Palmer," she muttered as she hurriedly cleared things away. "I'm leaving. I might be a few minutes early getting to Tall Tree, but I'd rather be early than late."

Removing her apron, she set a fresh pot of coffee to brew, then scribbled a note.

Heath.

The coffee is fresh and there are brownies in the pantry. Won't be long.

Theresa.

"Now I just need to figure out how to reach my cabin without being seen," she muttered, desperate to avoid any delays. "Shit. I can't. I guess I could leave from here. That's exactly what I'll do. I still have that lipstick in the glove compartment from the other night, and there's a comb in there too. That's all I need."

Worried about taking off the glove, and hoping the bleeding would stop during the drive, she left it on. Grabbing another paper towel in case it was needed, she moved quickly out the back door, climbed into the Land Rover, and rolled out of the motor court. Turning down the driveway she glanced in her rear-view mirror. Heath, Duke and Carly were in the ATV approaching the house.

"They left Andy to deal with Duke's horse!" she exclaimed. "I was right. Heath does want to set me up with Derrick Palmer. Sorry, Heath. I know your heart's in the right place, but that's not going to happen."

Accelerating through the gates and starting down the street, a wave of relief washed over her. She'd made it out just in time. Though her finger was throbbing, she paid it no attention as she sped to Tall Tree Farms. The familiar arched entrance soon came into view, and turning into the facility, she took a breath, slowed down, and forced herself to relax. A six horse trailer hooked up to Josh's white truck sat in the grassy area near the arena, and Josh was supervising the loading of several tack trucks. Looking at the clock on the dashboard she wasn't surprised to see she was twelve minutes early. Unable to suppress her joy as she neared the busy scene, she lowered her window and greeted him with a wide smile as he jogged up to welcome her.

"Hey, Princess."

"Hi. Sorry to be early," she said, quickly dropping her gloved hand from sight. "I needed to get out of the ranch or I would've been cornered serving coffee and cake to a visitor."

"Don't apologize. I'm pleased you're here. We'll have a little more time."

"Where should I park?"

"I'm gonna hop in and take you around back to the paddocks."

He marched around the Land Rover, then climbing in, to her surprise and delight, he leaned over, placed his hand under her chin and kissed her.

"Been thinkin' about doin' that all mornin'."

"I've had some thoughts of my own," she quipped, then immediately wondered if she should have made the flirtatious comment.

"Oh, yeah? You'll have to tell me about them."

"Not a chance," she said with an embarrassed giggle.

"We'll see about that."

"Tell me where to drive."

"Nice change of subject. Drive past the trailer and you'll see a gravel road off to the right. Just follow it."

Forced to raise her wounded hand, she prepared herself for the inevitable question.

"Theresa, what's with the glove?"

"Uh, nothing," she lied as she began to drive forward.

"Nothing? Then why is there blood on your wrist?"

Dropping her eyes, she spied the telltale red droplet.

"I had a little accident, but honestly, I'm fine."

"The hell you are. Pull up to the arena. I have a first aid kit in my office."

"I don't want to be any trouble."

"Then do as I ask. I'm puttin' on my instructor's hat. That means you do as you're told."

"But I'm not in training."

"You obviously need to be," he retorted, "or are you after that spankin' you asked me for the other night? Pull in over there."

With her stomach flipping, and her face flushing scarlet, she rolled to a stop by the entrance and turned off the engine. Her finger had begun throbbing, and she climbed out cautiously, not wanting to bang it as she closed her door. Josh had marched quickly to her side, and taking hold of her wrist, he lifted her arm.

"Keep your hand elevated. I didn't mean to be harsh, but you can't fool around with deep cuts," he said, his voice softening as he guided her inside the busy barn.

"I didn't mean to be difficult. It's just a bit embarrassing. Josh, there's a lot going on here," she remarked, spying his students in the throes of last minute chores. "Are you sure you have time for me?"

"Of course. What you're seein' is more excitement than work."

Entering his office, as he sat her in a chair in front of his desk, she recalled the moment between Heath and Carly in the kitchen the day before. When it came to Carly's well-being Heath pulled no punches. Theresa had found it sexy and endearing, and now Josh was showering her with the same attention. She loved it. She loved it so much she wanted to throw her arms around his neck and smother his face with grateful kisses.

"You're not attached to that glove, I hope," he said, opening a cabinet to retrieve a black leather bag and a hand towel.

"Not particularly. Why?"

"I'm going to cut it away."

"Isn't that a little dramatic?"

"Possibly, but it's easier," he declared, sitting next to her and wrapping the towel around her wrist. "Hold that." Using small, blunt nosed scissors, Josh cut the rubber glove, then cautiously lifting it away, he found her hand covered in blood. "I'm going to remove the paper. Because the wound has been under pressure, you might feel some discomfort."

"You sound like a doctor. That's the word they use when they mean it's going to hurt like hell."

"Yeah, well, that's because I was in med school for five minutes."

"Seriously. Ouch! Discomfort! Ouch."

"This cut needs stitches. It looks like you tried to slice off the nub of your finger. What happened?"

"I was dicing vegetables. The phone rang and made me jump."

"Damn, girl. Yep. Three should do it."

"Oh, great. I guess I'll need to go—"

"Nowhere. I can handle this," he said, cutting her off. "I'll numb the area, then treat it, a couple of sweeps with the needle, and you'll be done. Pick a spot on the wall to stare at, and talk to me as I work. It will make it easier for you."

"I can't believe you're able to do this."

"I come from a long line of doctors," he said, shooting her a wink. "Talk to me. Tell me why you went to the Horseshoe Tavern? Did you need to drown some sorrows?"

"Uh, no, I just wanted—ow!"

"Sorry. You wanted...?"

"A night out. Why did you leave med school?"

"I liked the science of medicine, but I didn't like the hours in the books. I thought about being a vet, but that had the same problem."

"How did you get into training?"

"Totally by accident. The instructor at the barn where I boarded my horse asked me to step in and teach the kids for a month. Long story short, I fell in love with teaching and I never looked back."

"Wow. That's amazing."

"Yeah, I think so too. There you go. Keep it dry, and the dressing should be changed in three days."

Dropping her eyes to study his work, she found her finger dressed in white gauze.

"Josh, you're a lifesaver. Thank you. Thank you so much. I'll bake you a batch of brownies. Everyone says they're the best, and they are, but I can't take credit. The recipe came from my grandmother."

"I will gratefully accept them in half-payment for my services."

"Half?"

"The other half is your company for dinner when I get back from the show."

"I'd love it. Can I meet Queenie now?"

"Absolutely," he said, rising from his chair and closing up his bag, "but I'll drive."

Walking back outside, they climbed into the Land Rover, and after pausing for a quick word with his workers, he drove down a gravel road behind the barn.

"I don't think I've been back there."

"The area is restricted for boarders. Helps to prevent strangers wanderin' in and messin' with the horses."

"That's an excellent idea. One of the things I like so much about Dream Horse Ranch is the security and privacy."

"How do you like workin' for Heath Boyd?"

"He's terrific, and I love the ranch and the horses. I especially love waking up to the quiet. That was the first thing that struck me. Not hearing sirens all the time," she said, a slight frown creasing her brow. "I never want to leave this peaceful life."

"Yep. Bein' in God's country—there's nothin' like it, though we have our share of drama."

As they approached a gate, Theresa understood why she'd been unaware of the pastures. A narrow thicket hid the paddocks and horses from view.

"The code is 1,2,3,4," he declared, pulling to a stop at a keypad in front of a gate.

Driving slowly forward, two golden retrievers bounded up to meet them, then ran alongside the car as Josh drove it to a parking area next to a large hay storage shed.

"That's Ben and Jerry, the paddock's official welcoming committee."

"Ben and Jerry? That's hilarious."

"Apparently they were holy terrors when they were puppies. Ice-cream calmed them down for five minutes."

"Who owns this place?"

"A real nice couple. John and Terry Coleman. They're older though, and I'm worried they'll sell. I knew the risk when I agreed to come on board, but I'm startin' to wonder if I should have passed."

"For the record," she said as he came to a stop and turned off the engine, "I'm glad you didn't."

"Yeah. Me too," he replied, grinning at her.

As she climbed out, Ben and Jerry demanded attention, and though careful with her hand, she crouched down and surrendered to their wet kisses.

"A word of warnin,'" Josh said as he joined her. "Don't throw their ball. They'll never leave you alone, and they're relentless."

"Ah, thanks for the tip," she said, straightening up. "Shoot. I left in such a hurry I forgot to grab some carrots."

"No problem."

Reaching into his pocket they walked to the large, fenced pens, he withdrew several bite-sized treats.

"Josh, these smell like peppermints. I want one."

"Queenie loves 'em. At Christmas she gets molasses cookies with a hard peppermint candy inside. I swear she rolls her eyes."

"That sounds good to me too. Where is she?"

"Just down here. She must be standin' in her shelter. You can see how they're back-to-back. I like that she's lookin' at the mountains and trees rather than the feed storage and arena."

"Definitely. I'm sure she feels more at ease thinking she's in the middle of nature."

"Yep. I'll announce our arrival," he said, bringing his fingers to his lips and letting out a whistle. "Here she comes. Theresa? Are you okay?"

But Theresa was speechless.

The big-boned chestnut walking to the gate sported a white blaze, a flaxen tail, and a roached mane.

CHAPTER SEVEN

UNABLE TO WRAP HER brain around the extraordinary sight, Theresa hadn't noticed Josh had turned to face her, and she'd barely heard his question.

"How is this possible?" she muttered, her goosebumps springing to life. "How?"

"How is what possible?" Josh pressed, walking over to her. "Theresa, what's goin' on?"

"I, uh, I'm not sure."

"Are you feelin' faint?"

"No, no, it's nothing like that."

"Then what is it. You're lookin' at Queenie like she's a ghost. Do you recognize her?"

"In a way."

"You're startin' to worry me. What do you mean, in a way?"

"I need to move closer."

"Go ahead, she's real friendly, but you've gotta tell me what's goin' on."

"Uh, I will, but may I have one of those peppermint things?"

"I thought you were afraid to feed a horse."

"I am, but not this one."

She was speaking softly, her attention focused on the mare, but when Josh handed her the horse treat, she glanced down at it, then lifted her eyes to meet his.

"I'm not sure how to tell you this, so I'll just say it. I had a dream last night and Queenie was a big part of it."

"A horse that looked like Queenie. Damn."

"No. Not a horse that looked like her, it *was* her."

49

"I was probably ridin' when you were here at some point and she stuck in your head."

"But, Josh, I've never seen you on a horse except that one time you got on Ranger and did a demonstration."

"Damn. I don't know what to say," he mumbled. "You're sure you've never seen her before today?"

"I'm sure," she replied, then shifting her eyes back to the mare, she walked slowly up to the gate. "Hey, Queenie, aren't you lovely? You're the most beautiful horse I've ever seen."

Opening her hand, Theresa offered the treat, and feeling no fear, she watched as Queenie's large lips gently scooped it up. Overwhelmed and fighting joyous tears, she moved her palm across the mare's neck.

"How long do we have?" she asked, as he stepped up and stood beside her.

"I've got about forty-five minutes before I need to do my final check and roll out."

"Is that enough time for me to sit on her?"

"Did I hear you right? You wanna get on?"

"I do. Just for a few minutes."

"You are full of surprises."

"Can I?"

"Are you sure about this?"

"I'm totally sure, and, uh...I don't want a saddle."

"Whoa. Theresa, you need a saddle. You'll be more secure."

"I don't want one. Really. I know she'll like it better, and so will I."

"Now you're startin' to freak me out."

"Why?"

"That's her favorite way to be ridden. She does best when I'm on her bareback. That's how I ride when I go out on the trail."

"Really?"

"How the hell did you know that?"

"Not a clue, except for the dream. In the dream I was on her bareback. I've dreamt about her twice. The first time I wasn't riding her though."

"No kiddin'? This is wild. Okay, let's take her into the arena."

"I'm so happy right now I could cry. This is a dream come true. Literally. Well, almost. Thank you," she said, impulsively throwing her arms around his neck and hugging him. "You're the best. You're the absolute best."

"I still can't believe you wanna get on my mare, but I'm real happy you do."

"I'm thrilled beyond words," she said breathlessly, pulling back and gazing up at him.

Suddenly leaning in, he fisted her hair and kissed her. As her heart hammered in her chest, she felt a warm flood soak her sex, and she wanted to be with him more than she'd ever wanted to be with anyone.

"I reckon we'd best get movin'," he mumbled in her ear, "or I won't be responsible for my actions."

Stepping back to catch her breath, she watched him lift Queenie's halter off the post next to the gate, step into the pen, slip it over her head and walk her out.

"Can I lead her?" she asked hopefully.

"I'm still tryin' to come to grips with your one-eighty, but here you go," he said, grinning broadly as he handed her the rope.

"I trust her. She's special," Theresa declared as they started walking to the arena.

"I won't argue with that. She's always had a way about her."

"What do you mean by—*a way about her*."

"All horses are sensitive. They're prey, and they're always alert and scannin'. They scan people, smells, movement, everything in their environment. But this horse, her sensitivity, if you wanna call it that, goes beyond the norm. Since the day I met her, she's shown an inklin' about things. Especially people."

"Can you give me an example?"

"Sure can. When I said, since the day I met her, I mean it. I found her at a feed lot."

"What's a feed lot?"

"A fancy name for a killer's yard."

"No! That's horrible."

"You'd be surprised the horses that show up there. Anyway, even though she was skinny and outta shape I liked the look of her. The foreman told me to forget it. Said a number of people had wanted to rescue her, but they couldn't catch her. She was starin' at me the whole time and I just had to try. He gave me a halter, I walked in the padock, and as I got close to her, lo and behold she walked right to me as sweet as could be. The foreman was floored. Couldn't believe it. I loaded her in my trailer, and she's never given me any problems."

"That's an amazing story."

"But even now, there are certain people she won't take a carrot from, and darn it if she isn't right every time. She doesn't do anything nasty, she just calmly turns her head and walks away."

"Oh, my gosh."

"Yep, Queenie's special, but how she ended up in your dreams? That's a question that's gonna be plaguin' me for a long while."

"Unless we get an answer."

"I don't see how."

"Maybe I'll dream it."

"Hah. Maybe you will," he said with a chuckle.

They'd entered the barn aisle adjacent to the riding ring, and while Theresa kept hold of the lead rope, Josh moved into the tack room to fetch the bridle.

"Queenie, I wish you could talk," Theresa murmured, gazing into the large, soft brown eyes. "Why were you in my dreams?"

To Theresa's surprise, the mare lowered her head and gave Theresa a gentle nudge.

"Oh, my gosh. You speak English. This is incredible."

"I think that sometimes," Josh remarked, walking up with the bridle. "I can ride her in that halter, but I think we should use this. Why are you grinnin' like that?"

"No reason."

"You're a terrible liar," he said, grinning back at her.

"All we're going to do is walk around the ring. Why do we need a bridle at all?"

"We need a bridle so you have reins in your hand, that's why. She's a special girl, but she's still a horse, and horses can—"

"She won't do anything wrong."

"Who's the trainer around here?"

"If you want me to answer that truthfully, I'd have to say she is."

Queenie snorted, sending Theresa into a fit of laughter, but when Josh started to remove the halter a second time, Queenie moved her head.

"Dang it."

"See?" Theresa exclaimed. "She's telling you she doesn't need it."

"How can I win with two women joinin' forces against me?"

"You can't."

"Fine. I'll compromise. I'll take the reins off the bridle and put 'em on the halter," he declared, but as he moved the leather rein through the holder, he muttered, "I can't believe I'm doin' this."

"We can," Theresa said with a giggle.

"Hey, don't push your luck, young lady."

"Or...?"

"Do it and find out."

"I'm not worried. You're leaving in thirty-minutes."

"But I'll be back, and I have an excellent memory. There. Done."

"I'm so excited I can't stand it."

"You be careful with that finger," he warned as they walked into the arena. "You could bang it gettin' on."

"Thanks for the reminder. That's just the sort of thing I'd do."

"One more time. Are you absolutely sure you wanna do this, and are you absolutely sure you don't want a saddle."

"Yes and yes."

"I still can't believe it," he said, shaking his head as he lined Queenie up next to the mounting block. "I'll hold her while you—"

But Theresa had already jumped on the platform and was swinging her leg over the mare's back.

"This is fantastic. I could sit up here forever."

"You're lucky she has a nice flat, muscled back. You ready for a walk?"

"*So* ready."

"It's gonna feel a bit strange at first. Any time you wanna get off—"

"I won't. You were right when you said you'd have a hard time getting me off once I was on."

"Watch that finger, and pick up the reins."

As Queenie began to move, Theresa let out a happy sigh. Completely at ease, she ran her fingers across the top of the mare's bristled mane.

"Why did you do this to her?"

"Her mane is thick and it's hard to take care of."

"I think she'd rather have it long and flowing."

"Dang it."

"What?"

"She gives me trouble every time I pull out the clippers."

"Why don't you listen?"

"I told you. Her mane is thick, and it's a pain."

"But it's beautiful, and she needs her mane. It keeps her warm in winter and the flies off her neck in summer."

"Listen to the expert."

"I read about it. Tell me I'm wrong."

"Why don't you enjoy your five-minute walk around this ring instead of arguin' with me?"

"I am enjoying my ride, a lot, and I'm not arguing, I'm simply saying having her mane like this might make life easier for you, but it's not right for her."

"I'll make you a deal. I'll let it grow out if you promise to come here and keep it groomed."

"Yes, please. I'd love that."

"Good. I'm happy and you're happy."

"And Queenie will be happier than both of us."

"You know you sound like a ten-year old on Christmas mornin'."

"Maybe because that's how I feel. When I dashed out of the ranch this morning I didn't expect you to be a doctor who would stitch up my finger, and I certainly never expected to be sitting on the horse from my dreams."

"And I sure as heck didn't expect I'd be walkin' around the ring with you sittin' on my mare bareback."

"You know what they say. Life's full of surprises."

"No kiddin'. You had enough?"

"Not by a long shot, but you have to leave, and I need to get back to the ranch."

"Don't worry. When I'm back from the show you're welcome any time. Okay, off now, but be careful not to bang your—"

"I know, I know, my finger."

Swinging her leg around and sliding down, she wrapped her arms around the mare's neck.

"Thank you so much, Queenie. You're amazing. I love you."

"I still don't understand any of this," Josh said, walking into the barn aisle and heading back to the paddocks. "None of it makes any sense. One minute you're nervous as all get out, and the next you're sittin' on my horse."

"This is a mystery to me too, but I don't care why this has happened, I'm just grateful it has."

"Amen to that."

"Josh, can I ask you something?"

"Let me guess. You want that spankin'?"

"Stop!"

"Don't you?"

"I swear, you're a one trick pony."

"Oh, no, Princess. I've got a whole lot more than one trick up my sleeve."

"You're impossible."

"So I've been told. Go ahead, ask away."

"One of the horses at Heath's barn dumped Carly yesterday."

"Huh. I don't know her personally, but I've heard she's one helluva rider," he remarked, putting Queenie into her pen and slipping off the halter. "What's your question?"

"The horse who bucked her off is no problem on the ground, but when anyone tries to ride him he gets nuts and throws them off."

"Is this Chuck?"

"You know him?"

"Sure. I saw him catapult someone at a show last year. I'd heard they'd pulled him from the circuit. I guess he ended up at Heath's."

"I don't know the whole story, but yeah. Carly got on him, and boom. Apparently he's been checked out from the bottom of his hoof to the top of his head. I just wondered if you might have any ideas."

"Ya know, I kinda do."

"You do? Really?"

"A few years back I knew a horse that liked chewin' on the wood fence around his corral. Real nice, easy fella. Out-of-the blue he got squirrelly. It was bad. No-one could figure why this horse was suddenly loco. Turned out he had a splinter in his mouth."

"No! The poor thing."

"Chuck's teeth will have been checked, but it might be worth gettin' in his mouth with a flashlight, or maybe usin' something long and soft to press around in there and see if he reacts."

"Josh, that's brilliant."

"Just a thought. Now I've gotta get movin'. You know where the tack room is. The treats are in the blue trunk with my initials."

"I know the one you mean."

"Everything you want or need will be in there, oh, and Queenie's stall is the second on the right as you come in from the paddocks. Her name is on the door."

"Thank you so much for letting me visit her while you're gone."

"You're doin' me the favor, remember?"

"Then it's a win, win. Bye, Queenie. I'll see you tomorrow."

The mare had been standing at the fence, and letting out a snort, she walked across to her shelter and began munching on the waiting hay.

"Josh, this has been the best forty-five minutes I've had since I arrived here," Theresa said earnestly. "Maybe the best forty-five minutes of my life. Seriously. I've had an amazing time."

"I have too," he said softly, and cupping her chin with his hand, he leaned down and drifted his mouth over her in a warm, languid kiss.

"Dinner when I get back."

"And brownies," she murmured, wishing he'd take her into his arms.

"And more kisses."

"And hugs."

"All of the above," he said, putting his arm around her shoulders and heading towards the Land Rover.

He opened the door for her, and she reluctantly climbed behind the wheel.

"Have a safe trip and a successful show."

"Thanks, Princess. I'll call you when I get a chance. By the way, you looked great on Queenie. Like you were born to ride."

"Really? I felt so at home."

"Yep. Really. Now go, or I'll stand here yappin.'"

Slowly turning the Rover around, she headed to the gate. As it swung open, she turned on the radio.

Luke Bryan was singing Most People Are Good.

She took it as a confirmation. Josh was a good guy.

CHAPTER EIGHT

DRIVING BACK TO DREAM Horse Ranch, though Theresa basked in the glow of her time with Josh, she also worried Duke Palmer would still be there. Turning off the street and into the driveway, as she approached the house and looked down at the open area near the barn, there was no sign of his trailer or truck. Relieved, she drove into the motor court and turned off the engine.

But she didn't climb out.

Closing her eyes, she sank into the memory of Josh's arms, and his delicious, devouring kiss. Her belly flipped, and a soft smile crossed her lips. She wanted to be naked with him, and she would be. There'd be no holding back, no second guessing, no game-playing, none of that. She would surrender herself without hesitation and let the chips fall where they may.

Her finger suddenly throbbed, but as she opened her eyes her smile didn't fade. The painful cut would leave a scar, but the thought didn't bother her. On the contrary, the evidence of the injury would remind her of his firm but gentle care. Sighing happily, she climbed from the SUV and walked through the back door into the kitchen. Josh had told her to wrap cling film around the bandage to prevent it getting wet, but as she took the package from the drawer and set it on the counter, Heath walked in. She prepared herself for the inevitable question.

"Hey, there. Lord, what'd you do to your finger," he asked, stepping quickly to her side. "Are you all right?"

"I sliced it making a Cobb salad for lunch, and yes, I'm fine."

"Too bad you missed Doc Briggs. He would've seen to it, but it looks like you found someone who knew what they were doin'. Did you run into the clinic while you were out?"

She hesitated. She didn't want to lie, but she didn't want a lecture about Josh either.

"Theresa?"

"The truth is, Josh Brady took care of me. He was a med student. He comes from a long line of doctors."

"No foolin'. Do you know why he bailed on medicine?"

"He said he had to follow his calling, and that was horses and training."

"Huh. Well, looks like he did a good job. I'm glad he was there for you."

"You are?"

"Sure. Is that why you hesitated when I asked if you went to the clinic? Were you afraid to tell me Josh put that bandage on?"

"A bit."

"Theresa, I told you earlier, it's your life and your heart, and I meant it. Your personal life is none of my business, unless someone mistreats you, then I'll make it my business, and he'll be sorry."

Her forehead crinkled. Except for the short time Henry had been in her life, as far back as she could remember she'd taken care of herself and Salvo. Her biker had been the only man who had offered her the loving support she'd seen Heath give Carly, but now, in his role as her boss and friend, he was offering it to her as well.

"Hey, I don't have all the details, but I know you and Salvo had it rough," Heath said kindly, his voice softening, "but you're not alone anymore."

"I, uh, I don't know what to say."

"Theresa, you're a remarkable young woman. You didn't let that bad stuff defeat you. You've got character and a good head on your shoulders. We're still learnin' about each other, but I won't judge you. I'm on your side and I'll look out for you. I'll tell you what I think, but your choices are your own, and if things go wrong I'll be here to help you pick up the pieces."

"I don't know what to say," she repeated, a wave of emotion sweeping over her. "I've never met people like you and Carly. And Andy too. How is saying thank you enough?"

Tears brimming, she stood motionless as Heath put an arm around her shoulders.

"You thank us every day by bein' here, especially when you bake."

His comment worked. She broke into a smile.

"I'm going to make you a rum cake this afternoon," she declared, running her hand across her cheeks to wipe away the tears.

"Sounds great. I've never had rum cake."

"You'll love it, but I haven't had a chance to ask you about Carly. How is she? What did the doctor say?"

"Nothin' serious. She's just banged up. Might've cracked a rib, but that's the worst of it. She's up and around. Said if she stays in that bed one more minute she'll have a fit, and I can't have that."

"What a relief."

"Yep. Now I need to get back to the office. I have a few things to finish up before lunch. Be careful with that finger."

"I will, and thanks, Heath. Thanks for everything."

"You betcha."

As he ambled away, Theresa finished wrapping her finger with the clingy, thin plastic, and with a happy heart, began preparing the midday meal. A little while later, as she placed the large wooden salad bowl on the dining table, Andy and Salvo walked in. Salvo raced to her side, peppering her with questions about her bandaged finger. After quickly telling the story, not using Josh's name but referring to him simply as a friend, Salvo followed her into the kitchen, offering to help her bring out the rest of the lunch.

"Sis, is the Land Rover open?" he asked, the moment the dining room door closed behind them.

"Of course, why?"

"I need to go to the feed store and I thought I'd swing by that house, but I need the directions off the navigator. I might spot the guy. At the very least I can get the address. Just describe it to me."

"Salvo, that's terrific. Let me think. I wanted to get away from there as fast as I could and I didn't pay much attention. The home was about half-way down the block. I do recall a chain link gate. There were steps leading up to the porch, and the top of the front door was stained glass, and arched. The glass I mean."

"That should be easy enough to find."

"I started the navigator at the end of the street."

"No worries. I'll find that house if I have to drive up and down the street a dozen times."

"You're the best."

"That's because I have the best sister any guy could ask for."

"This has been an emotional morning so you need to stop or I'll get all teary."

"Just sayin'."

"You're sounding more like a cowboy every day."

"I take that as a compliment."

"I meant it as one. I'll take the bread basket. Can you carry in the cheese platter and coffee thermos?"

"Sure."

Moving back into the dining room, Carly and Heath were sitting down and Andy was already helping himself to the salad.

"I spoke to Sandy," he declared, looking over at Carly. "She's happy to fill in until you're feelin' better. She's lookin' forward to it. I'm guessin' she misses her job."

"That's great, but I hope I heal fast. I feel so out of sorts not being able to ride."

"Have I met Sandy?" Theresa asked as Salvo came in and placed the coffee and cheese board on the table.

"She used to live in the cabin you're in now," he said. "She was the rider before Carly. You'll like her. She's really nice."

"Make sure she doesn't get on Chuck," Heath said solemnly. "We have two injured girls here. We don't need a third."

"Speaking of Chuck," Theresa began hesitantly. "Can I make a suggestion?"

Four sets of surprised eyes stared at her, but Andy spoke first.

"None of the experts can figure out his problem, so please, what's your idea?"

"Does he like to chew wood?"

"Uh...all our fences are plastic, and that's one of the reasons why," Andy replied. "Horses can't bite into plastic. I could call his former owners and ask."

"He does," Carly piped up. "He's in that paddock with the big oak and I saw him trying to gnaw at it the other day. Why do you ask, Theresa?"

"Maybe he has a splinter in his mouth, and he's fine until you put him in a bit and bridle. The vet might have checked his teeth, but an embedded splinter might not be visible. Even the tiniest splinter can hurt like hell when you put pressure on it. I'm not sure how you'd look. Maybe a rubber spatula? Something that won't hurt him if he—"

"Dammit, that's brilliant," Andy exclaimed, jumping from his chair. "I'm gonna go look right now."

"I'm coming with you," Carly said, pushing back her chair. "Ouch, I moved too fast."

"Heath, I might need you," Andy said, Carly's comment reminding him she wouldn't be able to help.

"Don't worry. If Carly's goin, I am too."

"You don't need to hold my hand every second," she quipped as he rose to his feet.

"Get used to it, 'cos that's how things are gonna be for the next few days."

The trio marched out, and Theresa and Salvo suddenly found themselves alone. When he heard the front door close, Salvo grinned across the table at his sister.

"Where the heck did you come up with that?"

"I didn't."

"Ah! Josh!"

"He knew a horse once that went from being easy to being difficult. The horse liked to chew wood and it turned out he had a splinter."

"Unbelievable. If Josh is right, you'll be a hero."

"Heroine, but they'll have him to thank."

"So, tell me, how did things go? When he played doctor did you play nurse?"

"Salvatore Cavalleri!"

"Sorry, I couldn't help that. Seriously, did you have a good time?"

"No, I had an amazing time. Are you ready for this? I sat on his horse."

"You did not."

"I did. She's gorgeous."

"Where did you find the courage?"

"I told him, and I'm telling you, but no-one else. I had two dreams about that horse. When she walked out of her shelter I almost fell over."

"That doesn't surprise me."

"What? How can you say that? I dream of the horse owned by some guy I just met, and it doesn't surprise you?"

"Theresa, you've always had that thing."

"What thing? What are you talking about?"

"You instinctively know stuff. The whole time we were growing up you always knew when dad was coming home and we needed to hightail out of the house."

"That was just—"

"Forget—*that was just!* He didn't have a schedule. We couldn't predict when he'd burst in blind drunk and in a rage, but you did. You'd be watching TV and suddenly jump and grab me. Don't you remember?"

"I've never thought about it."

"It wasn't Josh's horse making herself known to you, it was you, Theresa, seeing her. You were having one of your visions."

"My visions. Fuck. My visions."

"What's wrong?"

"You know what's wrong," she mumbled with a heavy frown.

"Henry?"

"Of course. That was the last vision I had, and I promised myself I wouldn't have any more ever again. Even though that jacket's a constant reminder of him, I pushed the vision far away. Remembering is too painful."

"Going on that ride was up to him. Your vision tried to help."

"I didn't try hard enough. I should have slashed his fucking tires. I've never told you what he said when he gave me his jacket."

"I know. I've always been afraid to ask."

"I was begging him not to go, and he took it off, handed it to me, and said if he didn't come back I'd have something to remember him by. Then he laughed."

"Do you think he knew?"

"I asked myself that question a thousand times, but there's no answer. He didn't listen, and he broke my heart."

"Maybe it's time to let this go, sis. Maybe you should trade in that leather jacket for one that's suede with a sheepskin lining."

"Maybe."

"Your feelings about things were good. Really good."

"I haven't thought about them in a long time, except the one I had about you showing up at my door. Two weeks later, you did."

"See! Don't you remember what you said to me the night we got separated?"

"No. I was in a panic."

"You said if we lost each other, not to worry because we'd find each other again."

"Shit. Why did I forget all that?"

"Probably because thinking back to that night isn't much fun."

"No kidding."

"What does your instinct tell you about Josh?"

"I've already told you. He's not the bad guy Heath has heard about. I don't know where the rumors came from, and I don't care."

"That's good enough for me, and sis, don't deny the visions. Look how they helped you today with that horse."

"Yeah. They did. I honestly thought Queenie—that's Josh's mare—I thought she was somehow reaching out to me. How crazy is that? You're right. I'm getting back in touch with that weird part of me. I guess I just didn't want to accept it."

"I'd call it magical, not weird."

"You calling something magical is magical in itself," she said with a grin, "but I have to admit I'm grateful for my dreams about Queenie. Was that the front door?"

"Yeah. They're back."

"Hey!" Andy said, walking in with a wide smile. "Dang it, Theresa, you were right. There's an area in the crack of his mouth where he's real sensitive. Can't see a damn thing, but put any pressure on it and the poor guy flips out."

"I feel like an idiot," Carly exclaimed. "I should've known. He was fussy when I put his bridle on."

"Like I said on the way up here, don't be so hard on yourself," Heath said as they sat down. "We had his teeth checked."

"I should've known," Carly repeated. "I feel so bad. Theresa, thank you. We owe you big time. How did you come up with that?"

"I can guess," Heath muttered under his breath.

"I didn't," Theresa replied. "The idea came from the same person who took care of my finger."

"Who is this person?" Carly pressed. "I want to thank him. More than that, I want to meet him."

"His name is Josh Brady," she said, a nervous flutter moving through her stomach. "He's the trainer at Tall Tree Farms."

CHAPTER NINE

"I'VE HEARD HE'S A REALLY good trainer," Carly exclaimed, then sensing an odd reaction from Andy and Heath, she added, "Is there something I don't know about this guy? Why do you two look like she just said she's friends with Jack the Ripper?"

"Don't be so dramatic," Heath said tersely. "Jack the Ripper!"

"From the looks on your faces, that name sprang to mind."

"Apparently there's a rumor that he's a love 'em and leave 'em type," Theresa said calmly, "and maybe he is, but gossip is just that. Gossip."

"I've told Theresa what she does in her personal life is none of our business," Heath said firmly, "but I'd be lyin' if I said I'm not concerned, and I'm sure Andy feels the same, but Theresa, you are right about gossip."

"Thank you."

"Duke was askin' about you today," Andy offered. "You could do worse. He owns that tavern, he's a good horseman, and seems like he's a nice fella. You know him, don't you Salvo?"

"No. I've never met him."

"You haven't? I guess you must've been out workin' the last couple of times he brought his horse in."

"Andy, I met Duke at the Horseshoe last night," Theresa said patiently, "and he does seem like a decent guy, but he's not my type. I truly appreciate your concern, really, I do, so for the record here's where things stand. I spent an hour with Josh this morning. He was extremely nice, he took care of my finger, and I sat on his horse. I had a lovely time. That's it. Do I like him? Yes. Will I see him again? Yes. And if something goes horribly wrong, so be it."

"You sat on his horse?" Carly exclaimed. "You actually rode?"

"Not rode exactly. Walked around the ring, and I loved every second."

"That's fantastic. If he managed to get you on board he's a thumbs up from me."

"I think Theresa has had enough of our input," Heath said firmly. "I'm ready for lunch. Salvo, would you please pass me the thermos? I'm dyin' for some coffee."

Grateful Heath had brought the subject of her love life to an end, Theresa scooped some salad into her plate. Though she had faith that her instincts about Josh were right, Heath and Andy's concern was unsettling. She'd spent every day with the two men for several months. They were men of integrity and she respected them tremendously.

Josh she barely knew.

IT WAS THE MIDDLE OF the afternoon. Theresa was carefully removing the promised rum cake from the oven. Her bandaged finger had been bothering her, and had made almost everything difficult. Her mood wasn't helped by the lunchtime conversation continuously replaying itself in her head.

"I wish I'd kept Josh a secret," she muttered as she placed the cake on the counter.

Turning off the heat, and ready for her afternoon cup of tea, she set the kettle to boil, and was reaching for a mug when the back door opened and Salvo entered. His flushed face and wide eyes sent her pulse racing. Something was wrong.

"Tell me."

"I think you'd better sit down."

"Salvo, just tell me."

"I went by the house."

"Shit. Who lives there?" she asked, closing the cabinet as a mug of tea became the furthest thing from her mind. "Did you see him?"

"I didn't see him, but the flag was up on the letter box so I knew there was mail waiting to be picked up."

"You opened it?"

"Yeah. Theresa, Josh lives there. You spent the night with him."

A strange prickling sensation moved through her body, her face turned hot, and an odd feeling of nausea filled her stomach.

"Sit down, Theresa. You need to sit down."

Sliding into a chair at the kitchen table, she shook her head in disbelief.

"No, no. He would have told me. No! This can't be right."

"I'm so sorry, sis. I really am."

"He said he wanted to talk to me more at the tavern, but I left before he could. He lied to me. How could I have been so wrong about him?"

"Maybe you're not. Don't jump to any conclusions. Not yet. Hear what he has to say."

"I'm such a fool. I saw him at the tavern with those girls. Why didn't I—?"

"Theresa, just wait before you condemn him. Hear him out."

"I feel sick. I feel really sick. I think I need to lie down."

"Do you want me to take you back to the cabin?"

"No. Yes. I don't know. Should I call him?"

"I think this is a conversation to have in person. You need to see the whites of his eyes."

"He's gone for a week. I don't think I can wait that long. No. I can't. I'll go crazy."

"Where is he?"

"Springdale. Do you know it?"

"Sure. It's not far. About forty-five minutes."

"He said an hour."

"Hauling horses, he's probably right."

"I'm going to see him."

"Theresa!"

"I am. I'm going to see him. I'm going right now."

"Stop! You're being impulsive. Don't do anything you might regret."

"I think I already have. This is a fucking nightmare."

"Shit. Sorry, Theresa, that's my phone," he said, reaching into his back pocket. "Hello? Hi, Andy."

As Salvo began his conversation, Theresa rose from the table, moved to the kitchen window and stared up at a slate grey sky.

"Queenie. I have to see Queenie."

"Theresa, I'm sorry but I have to go. Andy's waiting. Theresa, did you hear me?"

"I heard you. Go. I'm fine."

"Promise me you won't go to Springdale."

"I won't, but I am going to see his horse."

"Why?"

"I have no idea. If anyone asks where I went tell them I had to go to the store. And I will so it won't be a lie."

Hurrying past him and out the door, she climbed into the Land Rover and started down the driveway. Fighting the temptation to put her foot down, she rolled towards the gates, but once on the road she accelerated. Though the trip was quick, by the time she drove into Tall Tree Farm she was convinced something must have happened to the beautiful mare. That was the only circumstance that could explain the urgency pulsing through her. Stopping at the gate, she anxiously entered the code, but with Ben and Jerry bounding up to greet her, she had to move at a snail's pace to the parking area. The sky had darkened, and climbing from the SUV a light rain began to dust the ground. Praying for Queenie, she jogged to the fence, only to have her heart sink; the paddock sat empty.

Panic seized her, but only for a moment. All the pens were empty, but as thunder roared overhead she understood why. She'd left Dream Horse Ranch in such a hurry she hadn't grabbed her jacket, and crossing her arms she walked briskly to the barn, but before she could reach the entrance the skies opened up. The torrential downpour quickly saw her drenched, and finally staggering inside, she fell against the wall to catch her breath.

Still panting, raising her head she stared down the barn aisle. Except for the sounds of the horses the place was eerily quiet. After everything Salvo had told her about the ferocity of the storms she assumed the workers had fed the horses and left. She couldn't blame them, and as another drumbeat of thunder echoed through the late afternoon, she moved forward in search of Queenie. Recalling Josh had said her stall was the second past the door, it was only a few steps later Theresa found the beautiful mare calmly munching her hay.

"Queenie, thank, God. I've been so worried."

Lifting her head, the mare let out a soft nicker and ambled over to her.

"I'm so happy you're all right," Theresa mumbled, almost in tears with relief as she stroked the mare's face. "Why did you want to see me so badly? Or did you? Maybe I'm losing my mind?"

The horse nickered again, and sighing heavily, Theresa's heart began to settle.

"I'm going to get you some treats. I'll be right back."

Moving to the tack room, she opened the door, turned on the light, and walked across to Josh's blue trunk. The cold wet was seeping through to her bones, sending a shiver shuddering through her as she opened the lid. She was about to look for a towel when she spied a white envelope with her name scrawled across the front. Picking it up and ripping it open, she stared at the image of two horses touching noses. Not wanting to see the message, but unable to stop herself, she opened the card.

Princess.

As you read this I'll be tearing my hair out because one of my students is driving me nuts, or thrilled because someone has just left the ring carrying a ribbon, Either way I'll be smiling because I'll be thinking about you. I can't wait to see you when I get back. I'll bet those brownies will be delicious.

XO

Josh

"Is this some kind of sick joke?" she muttered, bristling with angry tears.

Tossing the card back into his trunk, she grabbed a handful of treats and stuffed them into her pockets. Her teeth almost chattering from the chill, and trying to ignore the raw emotion swirling through her heart, she marched down to Queenie's stall, slid the door open and stepped inside.

"Here you go, sweet girl. Treats for the loveliest horse ever," she murmured, holding them out in her flattened palm.

"Theresa?"

Her heart leapt, and for a split second she couldn't breathe, or think, or move.

"What are you doin' here?" Josh asked, entering the stall. "Damn, girl, you're soaked to the skin. You've gotta get outta those wet clothes. You'll catch your death."

"Bastard," she hissed, turning to face him.

"Whoa. What the hell?"

"Why didn't you tell me? Am I just a joke to you? I know what you did. I know I was at your house."

"Dammit," he muttered, a dark frown replacing the warm smile. "I can explain, but first we absolutely must get you out of those wet clothes."

"Fuck you. I'm not—"

She'd been interrupted by Queenie's nose on her back, but before she could react, the mare pushed her. Caught by surprise Theresa stumbled into Josh's arms.

"Thanks, Queenie."

"Let me go, asshole."

"Okay, that's enough," he said firmly, abruptly scooping her up and throwing her over his shoulder.

"What the hell are you doing?"

"What I have to. I don't care how hoppin' mad you are, you have to take off those clothes."

"Fuck you!"

"Where did that potty mouth come from?" he asked, marching down the aisle. "Doesn't suit you."

"I'm a city girl. That's how we talk to lying assholes."

"You've got it all wrong, Princess," he declared, opening the door to his office and carrying her to the couch. "I'll tell you exactly what happened, but first things first."

Plonking her down, he plugged in the heater, then opened a cabinet against the wall.

"There's nothing you can say to excuse what you did," she spat as he tossed her a towel and blanket.

"Take those wet clothes off and wrap yourself up. I'll be standing outside the door. When you're done hand them out to me and I'll throw them in the dryer."

"Are you out of your mind?"

"Let me put it like this. Either you take them off, or I'll do it for you."

"I'm getting out of here," she exclaimed, jumping to her feet.

"Nope, you're not drivin' in this storm," he said firmly, pushing her back down. "No way, no how, and you're not stayin' in those wet things. What's it gonna be? You, or me?"

The steely glint in his eye told her he meant every word, and though she hated to admit it, he was right. Her chill was growing worse by the second, and she had no desire to climb into the Land Rover and make her way through the frightening storm.

"Okay. But I'm only doing this because I'm freezing."

In spite of her anger and hurt she was grateful he'd returned. As he left the room, she quickly removed her phone from her jeans pocket, then peeled off her dripping clothes. Though they were soaked, she was relieved to find her underwear was only damp. Wrapping the blanket around herself, she padded to the door, cracked it open, and handed him her jeans, shirt, and socks.

"I'll be right back," he promised, then shooting her a wink, he said, "Don't go anywhere."

"Hilarious," she quipped, and closing the door, she returned to the couch, picked up her phone and texted Salvo.

Stuck at Tall Tree. Don't want to drive in this weather. Back when it passes.

Glad to hear from you sis. I was worried. Stay safe. Let me know when you're on your way home.

Will do.

As she placed the phone back on the coffee table, Josh walked in, and much to her chagrin, sat down next to her.

"Now we're gonna talk."

"There's nothing to talk about," she snapped. "I was told you were a player, but did I listen? No. How a wonderful mare like Queenie could pick you is beyond me, or was that just some bullshit story?"

"Theresa—"

"You lied to me. You fucking lied to me. You said you wanted to talk to me more that night, but I left before you could."

"Nope. That's not what I said."

"The hell it isn't," she shouted, her voice rising.

"I said, I wanted to talk to you more, but I didn't get the chance and that's the truth. I didn't say it was because you left, and I planned to tell everything over dinner when I got back."

"I know what you did," she growled, scowling up at him. "You drugged me. You slipped me a roofie."

"No, Theresa, I didn't," he said solemnly, shaking his head, "but someone did, and I got you outta there before that someone bundled you into their car and drove off with you. I was takin' care of you, Princess. I was protectin' you."

'

CHAPTER TEN

A HEAVY SILENCE HUNG in the air. Theresa knew Josh was waiting for his words to sink in, but even as her outrage began to subside, more questions surged to the surface.

"Why didn't you tell me when we had coffee, or when I came out here this morning? You could have called me. If someone's out to hurt me, don't you think I have a right to know?"

"A coffee shop? Not a chance. Wrong place, wrong time, and this mornin' was impossible. We had less than an hour, and I didn't wanna ruin what was happenin' with Queenie. But I had another reason for waitin'. When you woke me climbin' out of bed, I was about to turn around, but you were sneakin' away. You didn't wanna face whoever you thought you'd spent the night with."

"I didn't. I thought I'd left the tavern with a stranger. Talk about being mortified. I have been ever since."

"Princess, I'm so sorry," he said softly. "Would you like a hug?"

"Yes, please. Very much."

As he brought her into his arms and she sank into his chest, her anger and frustration evaporated, but guilt began seeping in to take their place.

"I'm sorry I misjudged you," she murmured. "I should have talked to you, not immediately thought the worst. Even Salvo told me not to assume anything."

"Salvo?"

"Salvatore. My little brother, except he's not so little anymore. I was just so shocked when I found out you were the man in the bed. I have a difficult time when it comes to, uh..."

"To what, Princess?"

"Trusting people, especially men," she managed, fighting the heat in her throat. "I mean, you barely gave me a second glance when I watched your lessons, then suddenly you came up to me in the parking lot and wanted to have coffee with me. I couldn't believe it. When I found out you lived in that house I freaked out. Nothing added up. Nothing made any sense."

"For pity's sake," he muttered. "I didn't look at you because I couldn't. You were way too distractin'."

"What?"

"You always wore that sexy leather jacket, your dark hair fallin' around your shoulders—I don't wanna begin to tell you the thoughts I had about your hair," he said huskily, sliding his hand into her long damp locks.

"But you'll tell me," she breathed, shifting her gaze to catch his.

"I'll do more than tell you."

Curling her hair into his fingers, he held her still, pressing his lips on hers in a passionate, demanding kiss, and to the sound of the pounding rain, the roaring thunder and the howling wind, he ripped the blanket from her body.

"Josh, I want you so bad," she panted, clinging to him as he unsnapped her bra and tossed it aside.

"Not as bad as I want you," he groaned, traveling his lips to her neck and sucking like a ravenous vampire. "I wanted you the first time I saw you walkin' down the barn aisle."

Abruptly standing up, he wrenched off his clothes, then sliding her panties down her legs, he stood back and stared at her nakedness.

"Please come back to me," she bleated, laying back and opening her arms.

"Careful with that finger."

"Screw my finger."

Stretching out beside her, he languidly drifted his mouth over hers, but pulled back with a frustrated grunt.

"Josh? What's wrong?"

"I just realized I don't have a condom. Sorry, Princess."

"Nowhere? Not in your truck, or—"

"No, dammit."

"I can't stand it."

"I swear I'm safe," he said fervently. "I don't mess around. That's why I don't have any."

"It's been ages for me. I know I'm clean. Please?" she begged, closing her eyes as he began roaming his hand over her body. "Please, Josh. Can't you just pull out?"

"Maybe, probably, yeah," he mumbled, trying to decide as his fingers slipped into her sex.

He clenched his teeth.

She was sopping.

Energy surged through his loins.

Grasping his manhood, he moved on top of her, placed himself at her entrance and thrust home, but as he began to stroke he discovered the couch was less than desirable.

"What's wrong? Please don't change your mind."

"I haven't, Princess," he crooned, sliding off her. "We're movin' to the floor."

Picking up the blanket, he flapped it out, dropped to his knees, then looked at her expectantly.

"You comin'?"

"God, yes."

Quickly sliding off the couch, she sprawled on her back and raised her arms. "Please, please,"

"Since you asked so nicely..."

Grabbing her hips and pulling her into his pelvis, he plunged into her depths and began to thrust. He had every intention of keeping a measured pace, but his fever seized him. The pace of his strokes quickened, her squeals echoed through the small room, then suddenly he felt his climax threatening. Sucking in the air, willing his pounding heart to be calm, he slowed his rhythm, finally coming to rest, staying buried inside her.

"Oh, my gosh," she said breathlessly. "That was incredible. Why did you stop?"

"Hate to admit it, but I had to."

"Already?" she panted.

"What can I say? That's what happens when a guy is on a diet too long."

As he released her hips and leaned forward to rest on his elbows, his muscled body towered over her, making him bigger than life. He was a conqueror taking her for his pleasure, pummeling her pussy, sweeping her away with his slow, powerful strokes. His torso brushed against her nipples sending scintillating pleasure through her breasts, and his cock caressed her clit with every stroke. In the whole world there was just him, and the glorious possession of her body.

"Don't stop," she begged, feeling the swell of her climatic balloon. "Please, don't stop, don't stop."

Determined she would have her orgasm, but knowing he couldn't last, he searched for an answer.

It came to him in a flash.

Nipple clamps!

Dropping his mouth to her breasts, he nipped as he thrust.

To his great joy and relief her body tensed, she held her breath, then with a loud shriek she exploded.

Continuing the tantalizing torment until her spasms waned, he straightened up, clutched her waist, and rode her until his climax approached. Quickly withdrawing and grabbing his cock, he spewed his essence across her stomach, groaning as the intense rush of pleasure pulsated through his body.

Breathless and serene, she curled against him, resting her head against the beating drum in his chest. Her sticky stomach didn't bother

her, nor was she worried about how much time had passed. Everything was right with the world. She had her very own, handsome, tough, loving, strong, sexy as hell cowboy.

"Hey, Princess. You doin' okay?"

"No, not at all. I'm miserable. I've had such an awful day. Especially the last—how long have I been held captive on this hard floor?"

"Aren't you just full of sass? If I wasn't so wiped out I'd spank that gorgeous butt of yours."

"Aww. Is this city girl too much for you, cowboy?"

"Keep talkin'. I'm makin' mental notes."

"You are? I'm so scared my knees are knocking."

"You're playin' with matches," he said with a grin, shifting to rest on his elbow, "and as much as I'd like to see you burn your fingers, I think your clothes will be dry."

"No, don't go yet," she pleaded as he rose to his feet. "Can't we sit up on the couch and talk for a minute? I still don't know everything that happened the other night."

"Yeah, you're right. I need to fill you in."

Helping her up, he grabbed the blanket, and settling next to her on the sofa, he laid it over their laps.

"Josh, I just had a thought. Why are you here? You're supposed to be at a show an hour away."

"One of my students loaded the wrong saddle."

"Don't you check everything before you leave?"

"She's fifteen and a scatterbrain, and yeah, I check everything, but this mornin' I was distracted by this gorgeous girl who wanted to sit on my mare. When she left all I could think about was how bad I wanted to be naked with her."

"I see. Did your wish come true?"

"And then some," he said, giving her a quick kiss. "What about you? Why did you come here?"

"When I found out I'd spent the night with you, I had the strongest feeling I had to come here and see Queenie, but I didn't know why."

"Dang. I could've called and had one of the workers bring the saddle to the show, but somethin' told me I needed to collect it myself. We were both compelled to get here."

"Josh, that's wild. What do you think it means?"

"Queenie wants us to be together," he said with a chuckle. "What else could it mean?"

"Queenie's special, but I'm not sure she's that special, though it is pretty weird. Anyway, getting back down to Earth. How did you know someone slipped something in my drink at The Horseshoe Tavern?"

"Prepare yourself, Princess."

"That doesn't sound good."

"It's not. Over the last year there's been a rash of incidents like yours, and they've all happened within a sixty mile radius."

"Seriously? Holy crap. How do you know about this?"

"A detective workin' on the case is a member of my gun club. He asked me to keep my eyes open. I've ended up much more involved than just keepin' my eyes open."

"Wow. Josh, this is intense."

"Yep. Intense and frustratin'. I wanna catch this guy real bad. I'm at a bar almost every night, but I don't drink. I flirt to keep up appearances, but my eyes are peeled every second."

"Oh, so that's why."

"Why what?"

"People warned me to keep my distance from you. Heath said you have a reputation as a love 'em and leave 'em, and Duke Palmer told me you're a Cowboy Casanova."

"Yeah, that's the downside. Do you remember seein' me with a blonde?"

"I do. You came in from the back."

"Everyone in that place assumed we were foolin' around, but she's a police officer. Her name's Wanda and we were comparin' notes. She's the one who drove your car to my place."

"You're kidding."

"When I saw you at the bar I almost came over, but I'd been watchin' this one guy, and you're—"

"Distracting."

"Yeah, exactly, but I kept my eye on you."

"Do you think he's the one who slipped the drug in my drink?"

"I dunno, but probably not. There were a ton of people there, and he'd already left when you came up and asked me to dance."

"I did?"

"Yep. I noticed right away you weren't right."

"How did you know I was drugged and not just wasted?"

"I know the symptoms."

"Oh, right, med school."

"That, and I've been trained. I hustled you outta there real quick, but I couldn't take you back to Dream Horse Ranch. I don't know Heath Boyd or your situation there. The last thing I wanted to do was wake up the ranch to get on the property, or let them see you in such a bad state. When we got back to my place we tried to put you in the guest room, but you refused."

"Did I give a reason?"

"Very loudly. I was your cowboy and you wouldn't go to bed without me. You're one stubborn girl. When you want something, you don't give up."

"Guilty," she said sheepishly. "Sorry."

"We finally surrendered. I left while Wanda took off your jeans and boots, but the minute she put you into bed you started yellin' for me. The minute I climbed in, you rolled against me and passed out. I didn't wanna leave. God forbid you woke up and found me gone. Lord knows what you might have done."

"I can't believe what I'm hearing. I'm so embarrassed."

"You don't need to be. It was the drug."

"Josh," she said solemnly, moving from the crook of his shoulder and facing him. "What do you think would have happened if you hadn't been there?"

"Not a pretty scenario. The victims wake up in out-of-the-way places. Picnic grounds are a favorite spot. Their clothes are scattered, and they have no idea where they are or how they got there. Any jewelry is usually gone, though he doesn't take their weddin' rings or phones. That's kinda bafflin. Like he cares."

"No-one sees him leave with these women?"

"This guy is smart and careful. He knows how to get them out of the bar, or club, or wherever it is, and he knows how to cover his tracks. And get this. He chooses bars with no security cameras. We think he leaves by himself, then somehow lures them out, but no-one can get a handle on how he does that."

"And none of the victims remember him?"

"Did you remember me?"

"I don't remember any of it, except dancing with you."

"That must have been when the drug took hold."

"I still can't believe I could have been..."

"Hey, you weren't. And you won't be," he said softly. "Here, you're getting cold again. Put the blanket around you and I'll fetch your clothes."

"I am feeling a bit chilly," she mumbled as he disentangled himself.

"We can't leave yet. That storm is still mad as hell."

"I don't mind. I love being in this empty barn with you."

"Me too," he said, leaning down and giving her a quick kiss. "I'll be right back."

As he left the room, she donned her underwear, then wrapping herself in the blanket, she walked across to the small window and stared out at the tempest.

"Hey, Princess. Watcha doin'?"

"Thinking," she replied, turning around to face him. "I have an idea. A really good one."

"Oh, yeah? Let's hear it."

"The guy who tried to nail me. He'll be pissed off and frustrated, right?"

"I reckon he'll be about as angry as that storm."

"I'm officially volunteering to go back to The Horseshoe Tavern to give him another shot. I'm the perfect bait."

CHAPTER ELEVEN

LAYING THERESA'S DRY clothes over his desk, Josh ambled word-lessly across the room. As he approached, her eyes danced with excitement, and shaking his head, he picked up her hand and studied the injured finger.

"I need to change this wet dressin'. Go sit in that chair by the desk."

"Didn't you hear me? I said I want to go back to The Horseshoe Tavern and draw out that scumbag."

"Yep, I heard you. Go sit down."

"But—"

"Go on now."

"Bossy," she muttered, padding across to the chair. "You could at least offer an opinion."

Moving to the cabinet and retrieving his medicine bag, he found the supplies he needed, then perched on the edge of the desk in front of her.

"Hand up, please."

"I take it you're not thrilled with the idea," she said as he began to remove the bandage. "I'll be perfectly safe. You'll be watching over me, and you could bring in your blonde police officer—jeez, for that matter you could have a bunch of cops there dressed like regular customers."

"I need to put more antiseptic on this. You might feel a sting."

"Would you please talk to me? Ouch."

"Sorry. Hold still."

"Josh, please. What do you think?"

"About you goin' into the tavern as bait?"

"Of course. Do you know you're being exasperating?"

"Yep," he said briskly, applying a fresh gauze bandage. "I'm makin' a point. I'm surprised it's takin' you so long to get it."

"And what point is that?"

"It's not even worth discussin'. There, you're all set. How's it feelin'?"

"I thought it would be bothering me, but it's not. Why are you so against the idea?"

"Theresa, I know you're stubborn, but—"

"Determined. I'm determined," she quipped, cutting him off. "There's a difference."

"Determined, stubborn, call it what you want, but you're not gettin' your way, not about this."

"Can't we even talk about it?"

"Didn't I already answer that question?"

"Now who's being stubborn?"

"I thought you were determined."

"I am. You're stubborn," she retorted, then taking a breath, she crinkled her brow and looked at him with pleading eyes. "I really want to do this. That dirtbag is out there hurting women. He tried to hurt me. Please let me help."

"Theresa, I'm gonna make this real clear," he said, pulling her to her feet and putting his arms around her. "There's no way I'm gonna be involved in any situation that puts you in harm's way. This guy is slick, real slick. There's no tellin' how he might turn the tables on us. The answer is absolutely not. No. Nada. Got it?"

"Uh-huh."

"Good," he murmured, leaning down planting a soft kiss. "Get dressed. I'll make us some coffee and check on the weather."

Stepping back, he picked up his supplies, dropped them into his bag, then moved back to the cabinet.

"If you don't want to help me catch this creep, I'll ask Salvo," she said softly. "He's smart, and he's got an amazing left hook. He could have been a pro boxer if he'd wanted to be. He'll be happy to be my bodyguard."

The threat had been an empty one.

A means to an end.

A trick to make Josh throw up his hands in defeat.

Placing his bag in the cabinet, he closed the door and turned to face her.

The glint in his eye sent her butterflies fluttering.

She'd made a mistake.

"You wanna repeat that?" he said, walking slowly towards her. "I wanna make sure I heard you right."

Her pride wanted to stand firm.

Her common sense said, back down.

Her pride won.

"Salvo. He'll be my bodyguard," she said, her heart hammering as she spoke. "This creep has to be stopped."

"Yeah, he does, and so do you."

With lightning speed he lifted his foot to the seat of the chair, grabbed her wrist, and yanked her over his thigh, but as he did the blanket fell away leaving her thin pink panties her only protection.

"What the hell?"

He responded with a sharp, swift blow to her sit spot.

"I dunno if you were tryin' to provoke this, or if you meant what you said, but either way you're gettin' your butt spanked."

"But I—"

His hot hand cut her off, and swiftly lowering her underwear, he delivered a flurry of hot smacks.

"You're not goin' anywhere near that tavern or any other bar," he exclaimed without missing a beat. "I care about you, and if you think I'm gonna let you go off half-cocked and try to catch a serial rapist you're outta your mind."

"Ow, ow, ow, stop, please, I'm sorry."

"You swear to me you're gonna forget this crazy idea?" he asked, pausing his hand.

"Yes. I swear."

"This is how I am, Theresa. I'm gonna watch out for you, and if that doesn't work in your book, I get it. Just tell me. Best we get this outta the way now. Are you okay with bein' spanked if I think you need it?"

A swell of emotion flooded her heart. Henry had been the same, and she'd loved every second of his take-charge, protective love.

"Yes, Sir."

"Have you been down this road before? Is that why you called me sir?"

"Yes, Sir."

"I can't say I'm surprised. I figured as much when you asked me to spank you at The Horseshoe, but we'll talk about that later. Right now we've got some unfinished business. You need to understand who you're dealin' with, and you've got a hankerin' to find out. Am I right? You want more? You need more?"

"Yes, Sir."

Her face flaming red, and her bottom stinging, she fleetingly wondered why she'd craved the loving authority Henry had given her, and Josh now offered, but his quick, brisk slaps snapped her back to the moment.

"Ow! Ow!"

"Yep, I'm gonna make your ass burn, Princess. You're not goin' off on some criminal chasin' adventure."

"I won't, I promise. Ow!"

His relentless, rhythmic hand continued to dance from cheek to cheek, reddening her skin and making her squeal, but he wasn't about to stop until he was sure he'd convinced her to drop the foolish plan.

"You sure about that? You wouldn't be makin' an empty promise, would you?"

"No, Sir. No. I won't go anywhere, I won't."

"You'd better not, 'cos until this guy is caught you're not safe, whether your settin' a trap or not," he declared, continuing to rain his hand on her scarlet backside.

"I understand! I do!"

He believed her. He also believed she understood who he was and how his mind worked, and to his great joy it appeared she still wanted him.

"Come here, Princess," he murmured, dropping his leg away and pulling her into his arms. "I had to spank you hard."

"I know."

"Anything you wanna say?"

"It was a stupid idea, and I'm sorry."

"What else?"

"Thank you. I've missed this so much."

"Yep, I can relate," he said with a heavy sigh. "It's been a long time for me too. I can't have what people call a normal relationship. But there's something else you need to say."

"How can you know me so well?"

"Comes with bein' a guy like me, I guess. Spit it out."

"I didn't mean what I said. I had no desire to go to the club with Salvo. I would never put him in that position, and I sure as hell don't want to be another victim. I was just trying to win."

"You win a lot, don't you, Princess?"

"Pretty much," she admitted, moving her head from the crook of his shoulder to look up at him. "But I don't think I'll be winning very much with you."

"That would only make you frustrated."

"It would, and that's so weird. Josh, my butt hurts."

"Good. I hope it stays that way for a while."

"Can I ask you something?"

"Sure."

"Why do you call me Princess?"

"The title suits you."

"That's it? There must be more. Or do you call all the women you're with Princess?"

"All the women? You think I've got a harem?"

"Maybe you did once," she said with a wink.

"I've never called any other woman Princess. Happy now?"

"No. Tell me the whole story. There's more to it. I can feel it."

"The storm's lettin' up," he remarked, turning his head to the window.

"No, no, no! You're not leaving here until you tell me."

"Who just got their tail spanked?"

"Pleeease?"

"Okay. This one you get to win."

"Yay, thank you," she exclaimed, pecking him on the cheek. "Tell me everything."

"There's not much to tell, but since you want to know everything I'll start with my mare. When I walked to the paddock and she turned her head and looked at me, I felt somethin'. Hard to explain, but I did. Like a jolt, and the name Queenie flashed through my head. When I first saw you walkin' into the barn, I damn near had a heart attack. You were wearin' that leather jacket with its shiny buttons, those tight jeans and high-heeled boots, and I swear, girl, you were a vision. When you came up and asked about lessons, your hair was flowing around you like a chocolate waterfall, and your dark eyes—I could barely look at you. I almost called you Princess right then. That's how I saw you, as a princess, and that's how I still see you, except now you're not *a* princess, your *my* princess."

"I am?" she whispered, a rush of excitement making her pulse tick up. "*Your* princess?"

"Yep. If you wanna be."

"I do, I do. That means you're my cowboy."

"I reckon it does."

"I'm so happy. I've caught myself a cowboy."

"Is that all I am? A cowboy."

"Yep. That's it. But you're all mine."

"You're somethin' else," he said with a chuckle. "I think I just bought myself a whole lotta trouble."

"Only the best kind," she quipped, then dropping her voice and moving her arms around his neck, she murmured, "A chocolate waterfall?"

"Uh, yeah," he said sheepishly. "That's what I thought when I saw it. I wanted to eat you up, all of you."

With a sassy smile, she moved her hands to the back of his head, pulled him down and kissed him.

"What was that for?" he murmured as they broke apart. "Not that you need a reason. You can kiss me any time you want."

"I had to. You've made me very happy."

"I'm glad, Princess, and I hate to say it, but I think the storm's lettin' up, but..."

"But...?"

"If you wanna sit on my lap, I reckon we've got five minutes."

"We may as well take advantage of the time we have left."

"Wrap your legs around me."

"You make that sound easy."

"It is. I'll help you."

With effortless ease, he grasped her waist and lifted her off the ground, and as her legs came around him, he carried her across to the sofa and sat down.

"First thing, we need to get rid of this again," he declared, unhooking her bra and setting it beside them. "Now put your finger against your clit and rub while I suck on your gorgeous tits."

"Oh, dear God. Do you have any idea how much you turn me on?"

"I'm startin' to. Finger against your clit, your good finger, that is."

"Well, duh."

"Hey, does your smart ass want more?"

"I plead the fifth," she replied, sliding her hand into her panties.

"Hush up and rub."

His hands clutched her breasts, and as he began to nibble her nipples, she closed her eyes and sank into the decadent attention. Her bottom burned, her heart pumped like a bass drum, and her drenched pussy sang to her massage. She would soon be crying out in pleasure, and dropping her head on his shoulder, she let out a soft moan of gratitude.

"You're gonna get yourself to the edge, then stop and count to five, then start up again," he whispered. "You only get to come when I say so."

"Yes, Sir."

Seconds turned into endless minutes. Each time he denied her, the need became greater. He pinched her sore cheeks, his lips devoured her neck, and his fingertips tweaked her nipples. When she finally heard his murmured permission, she exploded into a shattering orgasm.

"Remember that while I'm gone," he said softly as he held her. "When I get back we're gonna do that again, but you won't get to come until you've pleasured me with your mouth."

"I won't be able to think of anything else," she purred, "and I'll be counting the hours."

CHAPTER TWELVE

RELUCTANT TO PART, they kissed and hugged standing next to Queenie's stall. The bay mare had her head over her door looking for attention, and as Theresa slipped from Josh's arms, she fed the grateful horse the last of the treats.

"There you go, sweet girl. I'll be back to see you tomorrow."

With a soft nicker, Queenie turned away and returned to the large pile of hay in her feeder.

"She's so..."

"Present," Josh offered. "Some horses live in their own world, but when you catch her eye, she's right there."

"That's how it feels."

"Yep, and we're stallin'. We both need to hit the road."

Guiding her the short distance to the back entrance, they stared out at mud puddles and debris scattered across the grounds.

"Good grief. There's a lot of cleaning up to do," Theresa remarked, "and the rain is still coming down. You don't need to walk me to the car. I'll get through the rain faster if I just make a mad dash."

"Don't run too fast. You'll trip and end up in the mud."

"Good point. That's the last thing I need."

"I'll watch from here, then I'm going to follow you back to Dream Horse Ranch. The roads will be a mess. I want to make sure you get back in one piece."

"Josh, one thing," she said hesitantly. "Sometimes in the heat of the moment, or even after the heat of the moment, promises are made, things are said..."

"Whoa. Are you tryin' to tell me you don't want—"

"No! I'm not talking about me. I'm talking about you. If you find yourself thinking you jumped in too fast, I'll understand. When most guys say I'll call you they don't mean it, so if you start to feel—"

"Stop right there," he declared, pulling her into his arms. "I'm not most guys, and I've been wantin' to take you out ever since you first showed up here weeks ago. I told you that."

"But, Josh, you've barely said two words to me."

"You know how it is after lessons! I'm always racin' around, and there are too many people around to try to talk to anyone for more than a minute. I did look for you a couple of times after things settled down, but you were gone. Besides, how does a lowly cowboy like me approach a princess?"

"You're no lowly cowboy," she said with a giggle, "and I'm certainly no princess."

"Yeah you are, and don't you forget it."

"So—what made you come up to me at the supermarket?"

"The moment felt right, but now I'm kickin' myself for waitin' so long."

"You are?"

"You bet, but hey, things happen when they should, and trust me, I'm not havin' second thoughts," he said earnestly, then lowering his voice and looking at her solemnly, he added, "Theresa, I'll always be straight with you."

"Thank you, Josh. I needed to hear that."

"You feelin' better?"

"Yes, I am. Sorry, but I had to be sure."

"I'm glad you said something. Any time you're feelin' insecure you've gotta speak up. Imaginations can be deadly."

"I will. You're the best, Josh Brady. Okay, I guess I'm ready to make a run for the Rover. Wish me luck."

"Just be careful. I'll follow you to the ranch and call you when I get to Springdale."

Bolting into the weather, she dodged the puddles and branches littering the ground, quickly climbing into the SUV. Taking a second to catch her breath, she pulled off the waterproof parka Josh had lent her, then starting the engine, she turned on the heater, and slowly started down the gravel road. As she rounded the building, she spied Josh's truck with its headlights on. They flashed, signaling he was ready to follow her.

Keeping her speed down on the journey back to Dream Horse Ranch, her eyes stayed vigilant, and when she drew near the ranch she found herself navigating several downed branches. Finally reaching the driveway she turned off the road and rolled slowly towards the tall gates. Josh honked as he drove past, and honking back, she moved forward and headed up to the house. Evidence of the storm surrounded her, including the lawn chair from her back patio lying on its side in the middle of the lawn near the barn.

"Wow. This is a mess," she murmured, rolling to a stop, "but I'm so glad it happened. If I didn't know better I'd say that storm blew in just to bring Josh and me together. Thank you, weather Gods."

Climbing from the SUV, she hurried to the back door and into the kitchen. She'd made it back in time to prepare dinner, but found a message on the kitchen island from Andy. He'd left to spend the evening with Maureen and wouldn't be back until morning. Though happy as she'd ever been, a yawn swallowed her up, and as the weariness took hold, she decided to make pasta. She still had several jars of the sauce she'd made, so all she'd have to do was cook the linguini and pop some garlic bread in the oven to toast. Lifting a pan from the hanging kitchen pot rack, she filled it with water and set it to boil. She was pouring the sauce from the jar into a dish when she heard the doorbell. Not sure if anyone else was in the house she walked to the foyer, and opening the door she found a police officer on the porch.

"Hi, come in out of the rain," she said warmly, ushering him in. "Is everything okay? Did something happen?"

"Afternoon, Miss. I'm Officer Purdue. I'm doing some routine checks after the storm," he replied. "It was pretty bad, but you seemed to have come through it okay."

"Looks like we did, but I waited it out over at Tall Tree Farms. I'm Theresa, by the way. I just got home. Can I get you some coffee?"

"I'd love a cup. I can't stay long, but thanks. It's been a rough day."

"Sure. Come on through to the kitchen."

But as she started to leave the foyer, the door opened and Salvo entered.

"You're back!" he exclaimed. "I'm so glad. Why didn't you text me?"

"I just got home a couple of minutes ago. Officer Purdue, this is my brother, Salvo Cavalleri."

"Hi. Nice to meet you, officer. Is there a problem?"

"He's checking in because of the weather," Theresa said, "and you're dripping all over the floor. Take that slicker off and come into the kitchen. I'm making coffee."

"Great. Heath and Carly are at the barn with Chuck," Salvo declared as he took off the bright yellow raincoat. "The vet arrived, then the storm hit. They've been waiting for it to pass so he can examine Chuck. Not much fun having thunder banging over your head while you've got your hand in a horse's mouth."

"This sounds like quite a story," the officer remarked as they headed down the hall to the kitchen. "Horses, I love 'em, but they sure can have their problems."

"Have a seat at the table," Theresa offered, starting the coffee. "Salvo, be a doll and get the brownies from the pantry."

"This is real nice of you, and call me Jim. Officer Purdue is such a mouthful."

"Thanks, Jim."

He settled into the kitchen table, and when Salvo joined him with a plate of brownies, they began chatting about the storm. Producing steaming mugs of cinnamon coffee topped with whipped cream, Theresa sat down, but as she did the officer became solemn.

"There's something else I need to mention while I'm here. We're alerting everyone. We have a missing person. A woman. Her name is Claudia Harris. This is her picture," he said, unfolding a piece of paper and placing it on the table. "If she hasn't shown up by tomorrow morning these posters will be all over the county."

Theresa's skin prickled.

"Where was she last seen?" Salvo asked, just as Theresa was about to.

"The Horseshoe Tavern two nights ago."

"I saw her," Theresa blurted out. "I was there."

"You did? Please tell me everything you remember. Did you see her talking to anyone?"

Though she knew Josh was innocent of any wrongdoing, she paused, not sure what to say.

"Theresa, anything at all, the smallest detail might be helpful," the officer pressed. "Did she leave before you?"

"So, uh, where do I begin? Salvo, I planned to fill you in the moment I saw you."

"Fill me in about what?"

"You'll find out in a second. Jim, do you think she's another victim of the date rape drug guy?"

"I was about to mention that," he said, raising his eyebrows in surprise. "This is the first case in this town, but we've been anticipating his arrival. He's been broadening the net. How do you know about him?"

"I'm a friend of Josh Brady's. He told me."

"Ah, I see. You know you can't mention his involvement to anyone."

"Yes, he made that clear, but he knows I'll be telling Salvo and Heath. Does he know this woman is missing?"

"Not yet. It only became official a little while ago. Apparently she and her husband had a fight, and he thought she was just staying with a friend."

"Will you please tell me what this is all about?" Salvo said impatiently.

"We've got a psycho on the loose," Jim replied. "He's been targeting single women in bars and clubs. He slips them a drug, then somehow—and we don't know how he does this—but he lures them outside, abducts them, and they wake up with very little, or no memory."

"He takes their jewelry and money," Theresa interjected, "but he doesn't take their wedding rings or phones. The thing is, he leaves them in the middle of nowhere, right, Jim?"

"Yes, that's right. Sometimes they're ten minutes from town, other times they're miles away. But they have no idea where they are or how they got there. A grim scenario to say the least."

"I want to help!" Salvo exclaimed. "We have to find this guy."

"Believe me, we're pulling out all the stops, but Theresa, what can you tell me about that night?"

"I think I was supposed to be his victim."

"Why do you say that?"

"Because someone slipped something in *my* drink, and if Josh hadn't stepped up and helped me out of there, I might have been the woman you're looking for."

"You're one lucky lady."

"Very," Theresa murmured. "I have a hard time wrapping my brain around what might have happened, but to answer your question, the last time I saw Claudia she was talking to Josh in the parking lot. They were standing next to his truck. I went back inside and apparently that's when the drug took hold. I remember Josh coming back in and dancing with him, but that's all. He recognized the symptoms of the drug and hustled me out of the tavern. There was another officer there and she followed Josh in my car. Obviously I couldn't drive."

"That would have been Officer Herrington. She went back, but by then Claudia was gone. I'd advise you to be extra careful, Theresa. Cases like these can escalate. The perpetrator often becomes more confident and ups the ante, so to speak."

"Are you saying he'll come after Theresa during the day?" Salvo asked urgently. "That would be risky. Would he do that?"

"I'm not saying anything, I'm just speculating, but if he came after Theresa and failed, he might want to try again."

"I had the same thought," Theresa said, "but I didn't even consider the possibility he'd try something in daylight hours. Didn't all his victims come from bars and clubs?"

"Victims that we know of. There will be some who haven't come forward. It takes courage, and not everyone is prepared to face the ordeal."

"I have to help," Salvo repeated. "Tell me what I can do."

"When you're out keep your eyes open, and if you see anything suspicious contact us," the officer said, lifting a card from his breast pocket. "Don't do anything, just call."

"But what if I see a woman being bundled into a car? I can't just watch."

"You're a fit young man, but even those muscles won't stop a bullet. Take the time to memorize the make, model and color of the vehicle, and the license plate number, then call us."

"Got it. You can count on me."

"I can see you're eager to do something, but I don't think you should stake out bars and clubs. We're already doing that."

"Okay. I hear you," Salvo said, nodding his head.

"Time for me to hit the road. Thanks for the coffee and brownies, Theresa. They hit the spot."

"My pleasure. Take some with you," she said, rising to her feet and wrapping several in plastic wrap.

"That's mighty kind."

Salvo lingered in the kitchen while she walked the police officer to the door, and when she returned, she recognized Salvo's set jaw and narrowed eyes.

"Don't do it, Salvo. You heard him. Leave it to the police."

"The hell with that. I'm starting tonight."

"The Horseshoe Tavern is closed, and with the storm I'll bet the other bars will be too, at least tonight."

"Oh. I hadn't thought about that."

"How about this? I'll talk to Josh and ask him if he'd like to have you along for back up."

"Will you do that?"

"Sure. He's a really neat guy, Salvo. You'll like him, and I'll sleep better knowing the two of you are watching out for each other."

"That's a good plan. I like it. Thanks, sis, but I'm going with you when you run to the store until this asshole is caught."

"You won't get any arguments from me. I need the help. Loading those bags into the car can be a pain. I'll tell Heath and Carly about all this over dinner. Everyone needs to be on alert. This guy could be anywhere."

CHAPTER THIRTEEN

OVER DINNER THERESA had given Heath and Carly the details of her evening at The Horseshoe Tavern, explained Josh's covert involvement in the investigation, then finished with the visit from Officer Purdue and the disturbing news about Claudia's disappearance.

"Now you know everything," Theresa finished. "If Josh was in a bar and saw a woman leave alone, he made it his business to see her home safely. He wasn't picking up girl after girl. Unfortunately some were upset that he didn't want to stay with them. Perhaps that's where the rumors started."

"Carly, until this creep is caught you're not goin' anywhere without one of us along for the ride," Heath said firmly. "He could be anywhere, and who's to say he only does this at night?"

"Josh had the same concern," Theresa declared. "Especially with me."

"I'm not sure I'll leave the ranch," Carly said grimly. "The whole thing is so scary."

"I'm sorry, Theresa," Heath continued. "You were right about Josh, and you were also right when you said gossip is just that, gossip. I'm sure glad he was there for you."

"I am too, but I'm a bit worried. He should have called by now."

"He'll be fine. I'll bet he arrived at the show and found himself dealin' with a bunch of unexpected last minute problems. Happens all the time."

"I hope so. I feel edgy though, like something's wrong."

"Salvo, what do you have to say about all this?" Carly asked.

Theresa's brawny young brother hadn't commented, his expression remaining somber during the meal.

"I want to help. When Josh gets back I plan to go with him when he hangs out at the bars. I won't sleep until this bastard is caught, and I want to be the one who catches him."

"I said I'd ask Josh if you could join him," Theresa corrected him. "There are no guarantees he'll agree."

"I'm sure he'll appreciate the back up," Heath said. "I would if I were in his shoes, especially if that back up is you, Salvo. Excuse me. That's my phone," he muttered, pulling it from his pocket. "Huh. It's Andy. Hey, what's up?"

"A twister touched down in Springdale a little bit ago. Just heard it on the news. Hit the fairgrounds. I reckon we're lucky we didn't see one here. Seems like the storms are taperin' off though, thank goodness. Might've been the same cell that landed on top of us. Anyway, I thought you'd wanna know."

"Thanks, Andy. I'm glad you called. See you in the mornin'."

"Heath, what's wrong? Why are you looking at me like that?"

"A tornado just hit Springdale, but don't panic. We don't know anything yet."

"Where in Springdale? What aren't you telling me? I can see it in your eyes. Where in Springdale?"

"The fairgrounds area."

"I'm going. I'm going right now," she exclaimed, jumping to her feet as her heart leapt. "Salvo, will you keep me company?"

"Try and leave without me!"

"Theresa, think about this for a minute," Heath said, feigning a calm he didn't feel. "You don't wanna be—is that your phone? I'll bet that's Josh now."

Snatching it up, Theresa prayed fervently the caller would be Josh, but as she stared at the screen, her heart sank. The number was unfamiliar to her.

"No, it's not Josh. Hello?"

"Is this Theresa?"

"Yes."

"Hi, this is Sam. I'm the manager over at Tall Tree Farms. We've met a couple of times."

"Oh, hi, Sam. Have you heard from Josh? Is that why you're calling?"

"Uh, no. I tried to reach him but his phone goes straight to voicemail. He left your number in case of an emergency, and this isn't really an emergency, but I thought I should call. Queenie is upset. She's a real calm mare, and she's pacin' in her stall."

"Of course she is," Theresa said under her breath.

"Excuse me? I didn't quite catch that."

"There are some peppermint treats in Josh's blue trunk. She loves them. Maybe that will help. Uh, Sam, I'm about to ask you to do something, but please don't think I'm crazy."

"Most folks have some crazy in 'em," he said with a chuckle, "especially horse lovers."

"Thanks, and you're probably right. When you give her the treats, tell her you spoke to me and I'm on my way to see Josh."

"Sure. Be happy to. I talk to my horse all the time. I swear he understands, though sometimes he pretends not to, but why are you headin' to Springdale?"

"Apparently a tornado touched down and hit the fairgrounds."

"Say, what? That's why Queenie's agitated. Any other horse and I'd say it's the unsettled weather, except she and Josh are about as close as a horse and human can be. Is that why you're goin' up there? The twister?"

"Yes. I can't reach him and he promised he'd call. I need to know he's okay."

"I don't blame you a bit. Will you stay in touch with me? He's got half-a-dozen horses and students up there with him."

"Of course. I'll get back to you as soon as I know anything, and if Josh happens to reach you, please tell him I'm worried and to contact me."

"You bet."

"Thanks for calling, Sam. Bye."

"Bye, Theresa."

"Let's go, Salvo," she said, leaving the table. "I want to get on the road, like now!"

"Hold on," Heath said, holding up his hand. "I'm not happy about you takin' off like this. The weather's still bad. I've lived here long enough to know how unpredictable these storms are. I can tell you from personal experience, you don't wanna be drivin' tonight."

"I appreciate your concern, Heath, I do, but I'm going. I can't sit around here and worry. I'll go crazy."

"You should go," Carly piped up. "I'm sorry, Heath, but if you were in Springdale, I'd already be in my truck, but Theresa, I honestly think you probably haven't heard from Josh because the cell service is down."

"I think so too, and that makes it even more important I get up there. I'll be able to come back and with news about the kids he has with him. Their parents will be worried sick when they hear."

"And I'm sure some of them will hit the road," Heath exclaimed. "Theresa, I'm not happy about this. Not happy one bit."

"Maybe you're right. Maybe I am being an idiot, but I have to go. I just do."

"Then take my truck," he said resignedly. "Salvo, do you know the short cut around the back of the Johnson property?"

"Yeah. Andy went that way when we had to go to the hay warehouse on the outskirts of Springdale."

"That will cut at least fifteen minutes off the trip, and you're likely to meet road closures if you take the main road, not to mention the greater risk of downed power lines."

"Thanks, Heath. That's a great suggestion."

"Forty-seven Hilltop Avenue. Plug that into the navigator so you won't get lost. That's the address of the feed store down the street from the fairgrounds. The key's inside the glove compartment, and I filled the tank a couple of days ago so you won't have to worry about gas. Please stay in touch. Let me know when you arrive."

"We will, and Heath, thank you so much," Theresa said gratefully, then pausing, she added, "Do you think I should take anything with me?"

"Good question," Heath replied. "Food and water bottles. The truck has an excellent first-aid kit in the center console between the back seats, and there's a blanket rolled up there as well."

"Take my down parka. You'll find it in the hall closet," Carly offered. "You might need something warm and waterproof."

"Why do I suddenly feel as though I'm off on an expedition?" Theresa exclaimed. "I'm not traveling far."

"Have you ever witnessed the aftermath of a tornado?" Heath asked solemnly.

"Uh, no."

"Once you do you'll understand. You probably won't need those things, but you might run across folks who will."

"Oh, I see. Sorry. I didn't realize."

"No reason you should, but if you're goin', you'd better go now. The night's not gettin' any younger."

"Absolutely. Salvo, could you get the truck out of the garage and bring it around to the back door while I throw some stuff in the picnic basket? I'll be ready by the time you get there."

"You bet," Salvo replied, jumping to his feet and moving quickly from the room.

"Theresa, I've gotta say this," Heath said, rising to his feet. "You've only known this guy a short time, but you're headin' off like Carly here would take off after me."

"That's not strictly true. I've been around him at Tall Tree Farms for weeks, and we might have just connected, but he literally saved me. He got me out of The Horseshoe Tavern. If he hadn't, I'd be the missing woman right now. I owe him, and I, uh, I care about him. I care about him a lot."

"Heath, she knows how she feels," Carly said softly. "Time has nothing to do with that. Remember when we first met?"

"Yeah, I guess I do," he admitted. "Sorry, Theresa. I'm just concerned. Please watch yourself out there. Keep your eyes peeled and stay alert. And don't let Salvo drive fast. There could be all kinds of debris on the road."

"I will, and I love that you care about me."

"We do. If Andy was here I'd go with you, but I'm not leavin' Carly here alone, especially not while she's still hurtin'."

"I'm fine," Carly protested. "Go if you want."

"Nope. I'm not leavin'. Good luck, Theresa."

"Thanks. I'll call you soon."

Moving swiftly to the hall closet for Carly's parka, Theresa hurried into the kitchen and retrieved the picnic basket from the pantry. Filling it with packaged goods and a tub of her brownies, she placed it by the door, then grabbed some hand towels as an afterthought. She'd just finished when Salvo entered. She could hear the loud hum of the truck's powerful engine.

"Thanks for coming with me, Salvo. You probably think I'm crazy."

"Not even for a second. I'm glad we're going. I owe him."

"You owe him? Why do you owe him?"

"Why do you think? He took care of you. Now I'm going to make sure he's okay, and if he's not, I'll do whatever needs doing."

"Salvo. You're the best brother ever."

"We've already had this conversation, and we need to go."

"We do. There's a six pack of bottled water in that cabinet."

"Got it, but I'll put this in first," he said, picking up the picnic hamper. "You get in. I'll be right there."

Theresa had never been in the truck, and as she climbed up and settled into the passenger seat, the opulence of the cab surprised her. So did the view.

"I can see forever," she remarked as Salvo joined her, immediately putting the truck into gear. "We're so high off the ground."

"Isn't it cool?" he said with a grin. "I get that you're worried, but I'm sure Josh is fine, and I'm stoked to be driving this thing."

"You just made me feel better. Thanks."

"I did?"

"You're so sure he's okay."

"He's a smart guy. Smart guys do the smart thing, especially during an emergency."

"There you go again, being all wise on me."

"Just common sense, that's what Andy would say. Turn on some music. I need to concentrate. It's raining like crazy and I don't need to be distracted."

"Sorry."

The GPS led them through the deserted streets, and as they turned off the main route and started down a two-lane country road, the rain began to lessen. Lifting her gaze to the sky, she watched the clouds crisscross a pale moon. The minutes ticked by, and as they approached the end of the road where it turned sharply left towards the town the rain stopped altogether.

"Not far now," Theresa remarked as Salvo slowed and followed the sharp bend. "Only seventeen minutes to our destination. What are you doing? Why are you stopping?"

"Have you thought this through?"

"Salvo!"

"How do you think Josh will react?"

"What are you talking about?"

"You spent one day with him, and here you are, driving through crazy weather—"

"It's not even raining."

"Driving through crazy weather," he continued giving her a look, "to the scene of a tornado to find him. Don't you think that's a bit extreme?"

"Uh, no. Shit. Is it?"

"It could be seen that way. If you'd been going out with him for a while, no problem, but doing something crazy like this smacks of desperation."

"Seriously? You think so?"

"I don't know the guy, but it might."

"Shit. Should we go back?"

"That's up to you. Take a minute and think about it."

"But I'm worried."

"Like I said. Take a minute. How will he feel about you racing up here? This area sure is beautiful," he murmured, turning to look out his window.

"That's my phone," Theresa suddenly declared, grabbing her bag and pulling it out. "Salvo. It's Josh."

"That's great."

"What should I do?"

"Answer it."

"Shit."

"Answer, then decide what to say while you're talking to him."

"Right. Hi, Josh. Are you okay? We've been so worried."

"Yeah, I'm fine. Long story. I'm guessin' you heard about the twister."

"I sure did."

"What the hell is that?" Salvo muttered, peering out his window. "I'll be right back."

"Josh, one second. Salvo, where are you going?"

"I'll only be a minute," he said as he opened the door and climbed out.

"Theresa? What's goin' on?" Josh asked urgently. "Is someone with you?"

"Yes. My brother, Salvo."

"Where are you?"

"Uh, actually..."

"Theresa?"

"I'm just so happy to hear your voice. You weren't at the fairgrounds?"

"No, not even close. I'm boardin' the horses at a barn about fifteen minutes outside town, and I'm stayin' at a hotel about five minutes away. The twister didn't hit this area, but I lost cell service. Just got it back. Everyone else is stayin' in the center of town. From what I understand their hotel wasn't damaged so I'm guessin' they're okay."

"That's such a relief."

"What am I hearin' in your voice? Something's goin' on. You wanna tell me what that is, Princess?"

"I'm not a lunatic. What I've done might be a bit crazy, but I was worried."

"It's okay. Just tell me what's goin' on."

"Heath lent me his truck and I'm almost at Springdale. Salvo's driving, but he just stopped and got out. He said he saw something, but I have no idea what. Anyway, I heard the fairgrounds were hit, and when I couldn't reach you I panicked. So did Queenie. Sam called because she was so agitated."

"Wait. You came to Springdale?"

"I'm not there yet, but—oh, my gosh! What the hell...?"

"Theresa? What's happenin'?"

"It's Salvo. He coming back to the truck and it looks like—holy crap. He's carrying a woman. I'm going to run out there with a blanket, but I'll leave my phone on so you can hear what's happening. I'll be right back."

CHAPTER FOURTEEN

PLACING HER CELL PHONE on the center console, Theresa reached into the back seat, grabbed the blanket, and climbing quickly from the cab she hurried through the gusting winds. As she approached, she immediately recognized the woman drenched and motionless in Salvo's arms. It was Claudia Harris.

"Thank God you saw her," Theresa exclaimed, doing her best to cover the unconscious victim with the blanket. "She's so white. Salvo, is she, uh, alive?"

"Yeah. I'm no doctor but I'd say just barely."

"How the heck did you spot her?"

"I didn't. I saw this flash from the corner of my eye and I wanted to find out what it was," Salvo replied as they reached the truck. "She was on the ground. I almost turned around and came back because I thought it was just a pile of laundry or something. I guess I must have seen her fall. I want to put her in the back seat so you can sit with her. Will you get the door?"

Fighting the wind, she held it open as he lifted Claudia into the seat, then hurrying around the truck and climbing in, she covered Claudia with the blanket.

"Josh, are you still there?" she asked, grabbing her phone. "Salvo! Wait! Where the hell is he going now?" she exclaimed as her brother disappeared into the night.

"I'm here," Josh exclaimed. "Tell me what's happenin'."

"Salvo is running back into the field. I guess he must have seen something else."

"Theresa, who did he find? What's going on?"

"Has anyone been in touch with you about the disappearance of a woman named Claudia Harris?"

"Disappearance? I know who she is, but I haven't heard anything."

"That's who Salvo just found, and she's in bad shape."

"Damn. Tell me everything. How long has she been missing?"

"Since that night at The Horseshoe."

"How do you know about this?"

"A cop, Jim Purdue, came to the ranch and told us to keep our eyes open for her. Apparently she'd had a fight with her husband and that's why she was at the bar. When she didn't come home he thought she was staying with a friend. That's why he didn't file a missing persons report until this morning."

"Oh, no! Dammit. I can't believe this. I walked her out to her car and told her not to stop for any reason. How the heck did this happen?"

"I don't know, Josh, but don't you think whoever is behind these attacks must be known to these victims?"

"Maybe, but this isn't the time to be talkin' about theories. When you say she's in bad shape, what do you mean?"

"She's absolutely drenched, white as a sheet, and she's got a gash on her head."

"Theresa, you need to get off the phone and call the police," Salvo said urgently as he suddenly appeared, climbing into the truck settling behind the wheel. "I just found out my battery's dead."

"Hold on, Josh. Salvo, why did you go back out there?"

"To make sure there wasn't anything I might have missed. I found her bag," he declared, lifting up a wet, battered leather purse. "I know where the hospital is in Springdale. Call the police and tell them that's where we're headed."

"Theresa, I heard that," Josh exclaimed. "Where are you?"

"We just turned up that sharp bend that leads into town. The navigator said we're seventeen minutes from the fairgrounds."

"You're only five minutes away from me. Bring her here. The streets might be blocked off, and even if they're not, there's bound to be debris on roads, maybe even downed power lines. Turn right at the second light. I'm at the Black Stallion Hotel. I'll call for the police and an ambulance."

"Salvo, turn right at the second light," Theresa said hastily as Salvo drove forward.

"Where are we going?"

"We're meeting Josh at his hotel. Josh, we're on our way. One quick thing. After you call the police, get in touch with Sam. He's really worried."

"Will do, but Theresa, on your way here, see if you can get Claudia to wake up, and make sure she's kept warm."

"She's covered in a blanket, and I'll try. We'll see you in a minute. Bye."

"Why are we going to meet Josh?" Salvo asked as Theresa ended the call. "We need to get Claudia to the hospital."

"He was a med student. He'll know what to do while we're waiting for the ambulance, and he thinks the streets will be blocked. Salvo, slow down! We don't need to be in an accident."

"You're right," he muttered, taking his foot off the accelerator. "Damn. I can't believe I found her."

"Claudia? Can you hear me," Theresa said softly, tucking the blanket around Claudia's shoulders and wiping strands of wet hair from her face. "You're safe now. Wake up for me. Can you do that? Open your eyes. Shit. Salvo, I'm scared. Josh told me to wake her up, but she's not responding."

"Keep trying."

"Claudia, Claudia, open your eyes."

"I can't wait to get my hands on the scumbag who's doing this," Salvo grunted. "I swear I'll rip his fucking heart out."

"Just concentrate on getting us safely to Josh's hotel. It's called the Black Stallion. You'll probably see a sign. Come on, Claudia, wake up."

Though she didn't open her eyes, Theresa heard Claudia softly moan.

"That's it, Claudia. Everything's okay. Open your eyes. You're with friends."

"Ooh, my head."

"Salvo, she's coming around! Thank you, God. Don't worry, Claudia, you're safe now. Everything will be all right."

"Call Heath," Salvo suddenly said. "Let him know what's going on. He and Carly will be anxious."

"Oh, my gosh, you're right," she replied, quickly grabbing her phone and placing the call.

"Theresa? How are you?" Heath asked, picking up on the first ring. "I was startin' to worry."

"We're fine, but Salvo found the missing woman. The ambulance and police are meeting us at Josh's hotel."

"Did I hear you right? Salvo found Claudia Harris? How the heck did that happen?"

"By accident. We'll fill you in when we see you. We'll probably head home in the next hour or so."

"And Josh is okay?"

"Yes, he's fine. He's at a hotel on the outskirts of town. Apparently the tornado didn't get to this area."

"Thank goodness for that. Listen, Theresa, don't drive back tonight. I just heard the weather could kick up again, and even if it doesn't there's no reason for you to rush back here. I'd much prefer you make the drive in the morning. Where is Josh stayin'?"

"The Black Stallion. We should be there any minute."

"I know that hotel. I'll call and take care of the rooms for you and Salvo. I'll be able to sleep knowin' you're safe and not on the roads. How is Claudia Harris?"

"Uh, not so good," Theresa said, dropping her voice. "She's completely drenched, and she was unconscious until a second ago, but I think she's slowly coming awake. She was hit in the head. Maybe flying debris, or maybe her attacker. I have no idea."

"But she's alive."

"Yes, she's alive."

"I really didn't want you to go out tonight, but now I'm glad you did."

"Me too."

"There's no need to rush in the morning. I'm sure Carly and I can find the cereal and milk. You and Salvo just get back safely."

"Thanks so much, Heath."

"You're welcome, hon. Take care."

"We will. See you in the morning."

WITH THE POLICE AND ambulance on their way, as Josh placed the call to Sam, he made his way down to the lobby. Though caught up with thoughts of Claudia's surprising rescue, and hoping her condition wasn't critical, he was also coming to grips with Theresa's spontaneous drive through the stormy night solely out of worry for him.

"Thanks so much for callin', Josh," Sam said gratefully as he answered. "I've been pacin' around here like a nervous colt."

"I just got cell service back a few minutes ago. Theresa told me you were worried."

"How bad is it? Are the fairgrounds still standin'?"

"I haven't been into town. I'm sure the streets will be blocked and I don't wanna be in the way, but the local report on the radio said they were hit hard. Apparently nothing else was severely damaged, which is incredible when you think about it."

"Twisters are like scalpels."

"You got that right. Theresa said Queenie was agitated. Has she settled?"

"She sure has. You and that mare! That's some connection you've got."

"Don't I know it. Gotta go, Sam," he said, spying a hefty-looking truck roll into the parking lot. "I think Theresa just arrived."

"You take care now."

"You too. I'll see you in the mornin'," Josh said, ending the call, then moving swiftly through the doors, he jogged across to the impressive vehicle as it rolled to a stop.

"Hi. You must be Josh," Salvo said as he sent his window down. "I'm Salvo. Claudia Harris is in the back seat behind me. Do you want to get her inside or wait for the ambulance?"

"I wanna see her right away," Josh replied, opening the back door. "Hey, Princess."

"Hi, Josh. I'm so happy to see you. Do you want to sit here?"

"Yeah. That'd be good."

"I'll get in the front."

As Theresa climbed out, Josh shut the door, then hurried around and climbed in to sit next to Claudia.

"Hey, Claudia, it's me, Josh," he said softly, picking up her wrist and feeling her pulse. "Claudia?" he repeated, gently tapping her cheek. "Theresa, is there a first aid kit in this truck?"

"In the console beside you."

Quickly opening the compartment and seeing the black bag, he rifled through the contents.

"Ah, got it," he muttered, picking up a small paper package.

Crushing the contents, he broke it open and placed it under Claudia's nose. She immediately moved her head back and forth, then opened her eyes in a panic, but Josh was prepared and quickly reassured her.

"You're safe, Claudia. It's me, Josh."

"Huh?"

"Claudia, look at me."

"Josh? Where am I? Ooh, my head, and I'm so cold."

"I totally forgot. Carly's parka!" Theresa exclaimed, lifting the coat from the floor in front of her and handing it across to Josh.

"This is good," he said gratefully, placing it around Claudia who had begun trembling. "Slow deep breaths Claudia. An ambulance is on the way. Can you tell me your address?"

"Address? Uh—forty-two Crescent Drive."

"Do you have any pain besides your head?"

"Uh, my elbow and my knee. Tom. I need to call Tom. What time is it? What happened to me?"

"Easy. The police will contact your husband as soon as they get here, I can already hear the sirens. You'll be fine."

"I'm so confused. I don't understand what's happened."

"Claudia, listen to me. You're confused because you were drugged. Don't struggle to remember. All you need to do right now is take deep breaths."

"They're here!" Salvo exclaimed. "What should I do?"

"Jump out and wave the paramedics over here," Josh replied, studying the wound on Claudia's forehead. "This will need stitches, but it's not as bad as it looks."

"Josh, thank God you found me," Claudia mumbled, tears beginning to spill down her cheeks. "I was so lost."

"Someone else found you. I just happened to be close by."

The ambulance pulled alongside, and Josh gave the paramedics his initial findings. In quick order Claudia was placed on a stretcher and whisked away. The two officers who had answered the call, along with Theresa, Salvo and Josh, hurried through the blustery parking lot into the hotel. While Salvo gave his statement to one officer, the other sat with Theresa and Josh.

"I haven't had a chance to introduce myself. I'm Sergeant Kelly, and that's Officer Wyatt talking to the hero over there. We did receive the bulletin about the missing woman, but we never expected to find her up here," the officer said. "We're an hour away from where she was last seen."

"You probably haven't been told this, but I've been workin' unofficially with Officer Wanda Herrington on this case," Josh said solemnly. "We've been undercover for weeks now, but as far as I know, this is the first time the perp has hit a venue we were in."

"I was at the tavern that night too," Theresa volunteered. "Josh realized I'd been drugged and got me out of there, but I don't remember anything either."

"Are you suggesting this guy drugged both of you?" the sergeant asked.

"I'm gettin' an idea," Josh said thoughtfully. "Maybe he picks more than one victim, then goes after the most vulnerable. The lucky ones just think they drank too much."

"That's what I assumed," Theresa said. "I figured I'd downed one tequila too many."

"Whoever this bastard is, he must have seen me walk out to the parkin' lot with Claudia, then come back in," Josh declared. "He knew she was alone."

"We'll get to the bottom of this," the officer said confidently, rising to his feet. "He'll make a mistake. They always do. Looks like my partner is finished with your friend and we need to get to the hospital. By the way, where are you boarding your horses? I assume you were here for the show at the fairgrounds."

"Rise and Shine Stables, and yeah, but obviously that won't be happenin' now."

"Smitty's place. Sure. Good facility. When are you heading back?"

"Tomorrow mornin.'"

"Be careful driving. You'll probably find some branches scattered across the roads. I doubt we'll need you, but if we do I'll reach you through Wanda. Tell her hello from me. She's a good cop and a real nice lady."

"Sure will," Josh replied, standing up and shaking his hand. "I'll be here until tomorrow mornin' if you need me, and you've got my number. Call any time."

As the officers left, Salvo waved at Theresa, then gestured towards the reception desk.

"Um, Josh, Salvo and I are staying here tonight," Theresa said hesitantly. "Heath doesn't want us driving back."

"That's good. Heath's right. Why don't you join Salvo and get checked in. I need to call Wanda, then you and I should get together for a drink and a private chat in my room."

"I hope you're not upset with me."

"For what?"

"Coming here. It was totally impulsive, but I can be that way sometimes."

"No, Princess, I'm not upset. Salvo's wavin' again. Go take care of business. My room number's two-twelve. Knock on my door when you're done."

As he strode away, Theresa felt her butterflies burst to life.

"You might not be angry," she mumbled under her breath, "but you've got something on your mind."

CHAPTER FIFTEEN

JOSH'S ROOM OVERLOOKED the hills behind the hotel, and sitting in a chair by the window, he watched the wind whipping the trees as he placed the call to Wanda. Though she came from a long line of police officers, she was the first woman in her family to join the force. And she had excelled. Sharp instincts, calm under pressure, and a crack shot, she had won the respect of the department, but in spite of her skill, Josh's protective instincts would not be denied. Watching out for women came as naturally to him as breathing.

"Hey, Josh, I'm glad you called," she exclaimed. "I just heard about your busy night."

"News travels fast."

"It tends to when a missing woman is found. I understand she was rescued by a friend of yours."

"Yes and no. A friend's brother to be precise, and ironically that friend is Theresa Cavalleri."

"That's the young woman you took back to your house. I followed you in her Land Rover. Talk about ironic. How did he find her?"

"Sheer luck. He was drivin' towards the Springdale town center when he saw somethin' and decided to check it out."

"That's bizarre, but thank the Lord he did."

"Amen to that," Josh said solemnly.

"How is she? Claudia I mean."

"I'm pretty sure she'll be okay, but she was a mess. Besides being drenched, freezin' cold and sportin' a gash on her forehead, she was dazed, as though the drugs still affected her. That's one of the reasons I wanted to talk to you. She's been missin' at least thirty-six hours, and she's still out of it. I don't understand."

"Yeah. I've been discussing that with the captain. How could she be showing the drug's symptoms after so long? Do you have any thoughts?"

"Her confused state could be a result of that bang on the head, but I'm also thinkin' the perp kept her a while. If he did, does that mean he's changin' his M.O.?"

"Listen to you and your police jargon."

"That's what happens hangin' around a cop. I'll bet if you hung around the barn, you'd pick up a few things too."

"No doubt, but back to your question. Crimes like this often escalate. The offender gains confidence and pushes the envelope, though it's possible he decided this particular victim worthy of more time. We won't know until he strikes again."

"Damn, I wish we could stop that from happenin'."

"Sadly I've lost my number one suspect, and I'm not the only one on the force disappointed."

"I know you were sold on Duke Palmer, but I couldn't see it because none of the other victims came from our area. Not until now."

"Maybe that confidence I just spoke of is kicking in," Wanda remarked, "but it can't be him. Claudia disappeared leaving his bar the night I followed you home in Theresa Cavalleri's Land Rover. I was only gone fifteen minutes, twenty tops, and when I got back Derrick Palmer was still run off his feet."

"How can forensics have found nothin'?"

"That's the other huge question. How is he able to leave no trace? A hair, a fiber, something."

"Isn't that evidence in itself? Let's just go through this one more time and throw that into the mix. Dare we say this perp has police trainin'?"

"Keep an open mind. That's what my captain always says, so that's a possibility we can't ignore."

"I assume you've looked into Palmer's background. Is there anything there?"

"Nothing."

"But he was seen in some of the areas where other victims have been abducted, right?"

"Right."

"That's not much to go on."

"There's something about him that doesn't sit right with me," Wanda declared. "More a hunch than anything. This guy lives alone and he only works four nights a week. He has time to stalk, and there's no-one keeping tabs on him."

"I find it curious that he shut his tavern down for a week," Josh said thoughtfully. "Why doesn't he have one of his managers handle things while he's gone?"

"I can't let him go," Wanda exclaimed. "Unless he has a solid alibi for the last two nights he's staying in my cross-hairs, and your point is a good one. Why close up? How much money is he likely to lose?"

"Innocent explanation, he doesn't trust anyone. Is there a nefarious explanation? What could that be?"

"Excellent question! We don't have enough to get a search warrant, but I'm going to swing by the tavern tomorrow and check the place out. I'll drop by his house as well."

"Even though you know he was behind the bar the night Claudia Harris disappeared?"

"Yep. What you just said made my skin prickle. Claudia's car never left that parking lot."

"Wanda! Are you sayin' you think he kept her in the bar somewhere?"

"Just doing what my captain says. Keeping an open mind, but he's by the book so I'm not going to mention this to anyone. He won't condone me sniffing around without a warrant. I'll have to be careful."

"I'm a by-the-book-man myself, but not this time. I'll be home in the mornin'. I'd like to join you."

"Josh, hanging out in a bar with me is different from poking around a citizen's house. If I get caught I might be able to wiggle my way out of it, but I can't say the same for you."

"How about I happen to be in the neighborhood, and when I see you I stop to say hi."

"Are you sure you want to stick your neck out?"

"Hell, yeah, and I also don't want you pokin' around by yourself. Sorry, that doesn't work for this cowboy."

He could hear her grin, but a gentle knock caught his attention. Theresa had arrived.

"Do you think there's a chance Claudia will remember something?" Wanda continued.

"Hard to say, but I have to run. I'll call you when I get back."

"Stay safe, Josh, and I'm glad the twister didn't pay you a visit."

"Yeah, me too. It's been a wild night without addin' that into the mix. See you tomorrow."

"Bye."

"Bye, Wanda."

Ending the call, he strode across the room and opened the door. Holding a bottle of red wine in one hand, and her bag in the other, Theresa smiled up at him.

"I don't know if you like Cabernet, but I thought it fit the night."

"Sure. Good choice. Come on in. I think I saw wine glasses in the entertainment armoire," he said, closing the door behind her. "I'll take a look."

"Josh, before you do that," she began tentatively, "I need to say something."

"You look worried."

"I am. I know it was over the top jumping in a car and dashing up here. Sorry if I overstepped. I'm Italian. That's my only defense. I can be volatile sometimes, and unpredictable. Salvo accuses me of wearing my heart on my sleeve. At times like this I guess he's right."

Gently taking the bottle from her hand, he stepped across to the nightstand, set it down, then perched on the edge of the bed.

"Come and sit with me for a second."

Though she begged her heart to settle, Theresa's pulse continued to race, Salvo's words from earlier that night echoing through her head.

Doing something crazy like this smacks of desperation.

The gorgeous cowboy shared her love of spanking, and probably bondage too. She'd had a crush on him even before he'd put her over his knee, but now she was nuts about him. She couldn't bear to think she might have blown her chances. Telling herself she couldn't change the past, and regardless of what Josh said, she was glad she'd jumped in the truck and taken off. Claudia Harris would be lying in a field alone and near death if she hadn't. Taking a breath, consoled by the good that had come from her impetuous decision, she walked to Josh, dropped her bag on the floor, and settled next to him.

"Funny thing, when I said I wanted to talk to you, this is exactly why. I must admit, when you first said you'd left the ranch 'cos you heard about the tornado and wanted to make sure I was okay, it kinda shocked me."

"I didn't mean to—"

"Hush up. I haven't finished. After the surprise wore off I started thinkin'. One of the things that drives me crazy, and probably most other men too, is when a girl thinks she's gotta play head games. There's nothin' attractive about dishonesty, and that includes the playin' hard to get thing. What you did tonight was about as honest as honest gets. A bit crazy, sure, but you weren't afraid to show you cared. That counts for a whole lot in my book, and you know what? If I'd been here and heard a twister had hit back home and I couldn't reach you, I would've jumped in my truck and tried to find you."

"Really?"

"In a heartbeat. I'm flattered that you came out here, and look at the good that came out of it. Because you threw away any worry about what I might think, you probably saved a life. At the very least you rescued a woman from more hours of suffering, and put her loved ones out of their misery."

"Josh, thank you," she said gratefully, throwing her arms around his neck. "You're the best. You're the absolute best."

"I reckon I'm sharin' that title with you, Princess," he softly replied, hugging her tightly. "I know you've got your own room, but there's no way I'm lettin' you leave."

"Salvo will be happy."

"How's that?"

"With the fair supposed to be starting tomorrow, the hotel had only one room left. Salvo won't have to sleep on the floor. I'd better text him and let him know."

"Seems like everyone's comin' out on top tonight, includin' Springdale. Last report I heard there are only minor injuries. The fairground was hit, but that's it. I guess the twister touched down, then scurried outta here."

"I've never seen a tornado and I'm not sure I want to."

"They're monsters, but they sure are breathtakin' to look at. You contact Salvo and I'll open the wine."

"Are you hungry? There's a picnic hamper in the truck, and guess what's in it?"

"I'm too distracted lookin' at you to play guessin' games," he murmured, lifting her hair and kissing her neck, "except maybe thinkin' about what you're wearin' under these clothes."

"Brownies."

"Mmm, they'd go real good with red wine. How do we get 'em without leavin' the room?"

"I'll ask Salvo to fetch them for me."

"Good plan. Your little brother is handy."

"Yeah. He can be."

"Here's the plan. You text him, give him the good news, then send him on the errand. While you're doin' that I'm gonna start the tub. You and I are gonna soak in hot foam for a while."

"Ooh, that sounds heavenly."

"And I think I might have to tan your tail."

"Why?"

"A whole lotta good came outta tonight, but you were still reckless."

"You're just looking for an excuse."

"I don't need an excuse. You've got a mighty spankable ass."

"Aww, thanks, cowboy, uh, I think."

"Text Salvo before I rip your clothes off."

Giggling as she reached down and picked up her bag, she rummaged through the contents and retrieved her phone.

"By the way, how's the finger?" he asked, watching her touch the keypad with only the forefinger of her right hand.

"It hardly bothers me at all. I had an exceptional doctor."

"Glad to hear it."

"There. Done! Salvo will be knocking on the door any minute with the brownies."

"We need to make sure it doesn't get wet in the tub."

"I assume you're talking about my finger. What would you suggest?"

"I have an idea," he replied with a wicked grin. "Yep, I have the very thing."

"Why am I suddenly feeling you have something devilish in mind?"

"Because I do, Princess, and before you ask, no, I won't tell you. You'll just have to wait and find out."

AS THEY WALKED DOWN the hospital corridor toward the exit, young Officer Fred Wyatt and Sergeant Dustin Kelly were deep in conversation. The doctors had allowed them only a brief visit with Claudia Harris. Though conscious, suffering from exposure, shock, and concussion, the woman desperately needed rest.

"You know what I can't stop thinking about?" the young officer said solemnly. "Josh Brady was the last person to see that woman, and he's here, right where she was found. He arrived this morning, right?"

"Huh. That's right."

"Isn't that too much of a coincidence to ignore?"

"You know, you might have something there."

"What should we do? Check out his truck?"

"This perp is smart, and if it's Josh Brady he sure wouldn't leave anything sitting on the passenger seat, and we sure can't open it up without a warrant. His horse trailer though, that might be worth a look-see. If it's parked on Smitty's property and he gives us permission to take a look, we're good."

"Even though the trailer belongs to Josh Brady."

"Yep, even though the trailer belongs to Josh Brady. Good thinking, Fred. Let's head on over there!"

CHAPTER SIXTEEN

PROPPED UP ON THE BED drinking a glass of red wine while they waited for the tub to fill, Josh fed Theresa a piece of brownie, then popped the remainder in his mouth. As the delicious decadence dissolved against his tongue, he rolled his eyes in pleasure.

"Theresa, this is sinful."

With the gooey richness muffling his speech he'd barely managed the words, but leaning forward he pressed his lips on hers and shared the chocolatey wonder.

"Of all the times I've enjoyed my grandmother's brownies, that was the best," she murmured softly, then taking a sip of her wine, she sank back and released a happy sigh. "I'm beginning to feel almost human again."

"You sit there for a minute. I'm gonna check the water."

"I'm not sure I'd be able to move anyway. I'm totally exhausted."

"I'll bet you are," he remarked. "Drink your wine. You need to chill."

Climbing from the bed and ambling into the bathroom, though the bubbles sat at the top, when he lowered his arm into the aromatic suds he found the tub half-full. With both of them in the bath, any higher and the water would splash over the sides. Turning off the faucets, he walked back to the bed and perched on the edge of the mattress.

"Hey, Princess, you wanna join me in a soak, or has that wine got the better of you?"

"The soak. Definitely. I feel covered in crap."

"Yeah, the wind makes you feel that way."

"I can't wait to feel clean again."

"I should warn you, I've gotta surprise waitin."

"I consider myself warned," she said with a grin. "Do with me as you will."

"I intend to, and I'm gonna start by takin' off your clothes. You don't do a thing. Got it?"

"Yes, Sir."

Slowly peeling off the layers, as he placed her belongings neatly on the chair by the window, he could feel her eyes on him.

"What?" he asked as he returned to pop the snap on her bra.

"I don't understand the question."

"You were staring at me."

"You're easy on the eyes," she said with a giggle. "I think I'm getting a bit buzzed."

"Thank you, Princess, but that's not the feelin' I was gettin.'"

"Watching you put my stuff on the chair reminded me of the morning I woke up at your house."

"Yeah, I can see why."

"You're awfully neat for a cowboy," she remarked, as he shimmied her panties down her legs.

"I didn't know cowboys had a reputation for bein' messy."

"Good point."

"Wineglass on the nightstand," he commanded. "Tub time." Waiting until the glass had been safely set in place, he effortlessly lifted her up, and carrying her into the bathroom he stood her on her feet in the warm, soapy water. "Lay back with your head below the faucets and raise your arms."

"What are you going to do?"

"You'll find out. Just do as I ask."

As she lowered herself into the foam, he removed the sash from the bathrobe supplied by the hotel, then tying her wrists together, he looped the sash around the faucets. "Perfect. You look a treat, Princess."

With the aromatic suds floating around her body, Theresa gazed up at the handsome cowboy leaning over her. Wearing a devilish grin, he slowly peeled off his shirt, then his trousers and boxers.

"Someone's happy to see me," she said, staring at his cock standing proudly at attention. "Too bad I can't give him an appropriate welcome, like shaking his hand, or giving him a wet, sloppy kiss."

"You'll be able to bring out the welcoming committee soon, but you'll stay as you are for the moment."

"Don't you want him to enjoy my attention?" she asked, her eyes twinkling up at him.

"Are you sayin' you don't like bein' at my mercy?"

"You're answering my question with another question."

"Yep, and I'm gonna ask again, and this time I want an answer. Do you like bein' at my mercy?"

"I haven't made up my mind yet," she said flippantly, raising her eyebrows. "I suppose my answer will depend on what you plan on doing to this helpless female."

"Damn, girl, you're in one sassy mood," he remarked, kneeling beside the tub and sliding his hand over her breasts. "You might wanna think twice about pushin' your luck."

"If that's what I'm doing, blame the wine."

"The wine? Uh-uh. You know exactly what you're doin', and that's askin' me to take you in hand."

"Take me in hand? Ooh, that is so sexy."

"You think?" he purred, leaning down and softly sucking on her neck. "If you ever wanna feel my belt kiss your butt, you go right ahead and keep on pushin'."

"Call me crazy, but there's a part of me that wants to accept that challenge."

Her breathless words brought a fresh grin to his lips.

"Don't think I wouldn't do it," he warned, lifting his head and fixing her with a steady gaze, "but we'll talk about that later. Do you want my company in that warm soapy water?"

"Of course."

"Yeah, then ask nice!"

"I have to ask?"

"You sure do, Princess, and be grateful. With all that sass I could've walked away and left you tied up in there."

"Josh! Not tonight. You wouldn't do something like that tonight!"

"No, not tonight, but remember that promise, and you still have to ask nicely."

"Please, Sir, will you keep me company in this lovely bath?"

"That's my girl," he said softly, pecking the tip of her nose.

Climbing into the opposite end of the tub, he stretched out his legs on either side of hers, then laid back and let out a heavy sigh.

"Man this feels good. Whatta day."

"Who would have thought you're a cowboy who likes a bubble bath?"

"I can't imagine a cowboy who wouldn't with you in the tub."

"Good answer."

Sitting up, he moved his hands against her slippery inner thighs, then slowly slid them towards her pussy. As she closed her eyes, he heard a soft, quick intake of breath. Though he knew she ached for his fingers to explore between her legs, he traveled his caress past her sex and over her belly.

"Josh, please touch me?"

"I am touchin' you."

"You know what I mean."

"Not yet, Princess."

Moving his hands to her nipples, he lightly tweaked, then tweaked again—harder—but her yelp quickly faded as he began kneading her breasts.

"You sure have beautiful tits. I can't wait to lace 'em with my rope. Have you ever been laced, Princess?"

"A bit," she managed between moans.

"You wanna try for more than a bit?"

"Yes, Sir."

"Ah, behavin' now are we? What happened to that sassy girl who was here a few minutes ago?"

"I banished her."

"Because?"

"Because I need you. I'll be good, I swear. I want you so bad I can't stand it."

Slowly sitting back, he drifted his hands back down her body and slipped his fingers into her womanhood. Even in the scented water he could feel her slick moisture, and massaging his thumb against her clit, he pushed a finger into her depths.

"Sir, please don't stop."

"Let me know when you're on the edge, but don't you dare come. You hear me?"

"Ooh, Sir, I'll try not to."

"Try? That's not good enough," he warned as he stroked her faster and rubbed more aggressively. "You'd better tell me."

"Yes, Sir."

She'd panted her reply, and though his cock was screaming for attention, he watched her closely, studying the rise and fall of her chest as her gasps and moans continued to rise in pitch.

"Sir, I'm almost there," she suddenly wailed. "I can feel it."

"Good girl," he said softly, immediately withdrawing his hand. "Now you just lie there and relax for a minute."

"Relax? How can I relax?" she whined, squirming and sending water over the edge of the tub.

"Take a deep breath, and don't worry, I won't leave you hangin' for long."

Taking his member in his hand and enjoying the sight of her glossy nakedness, he stroked himself and pondered a decision; mutual masturbation in the bath, or lift her out, dry her off and ravage her on the bed? Deciding on the latter, he released his cock and lifted the soft sponge from the built-in shelf.

"How long will you make me wait?" she bleated, her eyes half-lidded.

"A little bit longer every time you ask. Close your eyes. This is gonna feel real good."

With a resigned sigh she did as he instructed, and as he glided the soft sponge across her chest and up her arms, he was rewarded with a series of sensuous moans. It had been years since he'd bathed a beautiful woman, and though he relished every moment, his craving for her finally won out.

"Okay, Princess. After I untie you I want you to kneel, and watch that finger."

"Why?"

"Why? Because I said so."

"Why more than that?"

"You really are feelin' that wine," he said with a chuckle as he leaned over and undid the knot. "There you go."

"I guess I am, but I still want to know."

"I'm gonna wash your back, then we're takin' this to the bed."

"Yummy."

"You're a kick when you're a bit buzzed."

Moving the sponge across her shoulders, down her back and over her bottom, he quickly slipped it between her cheeks. To his surprise she didn't react, but calmly accepted the decadent attention. Placing the sponge back on the shelf, he stepped out and offered his hand.

"Come on, darlin', take your time."

"I know how to get out of a tub!"

"You can be such a brat. Not to worry. I'll soon fix that."

With her safely out of the water, he dried her off and ran the towel over his body, then swooping her up, he carried her through to the bed.

"On to your elbows and knees," he declared, laying her on her stomach and climbing on the mattress behind her.

He waited, but she mumbled something he couldn't make out and remained motionless.

"I didn't hear you."

Looking at him over her shoulder, she grinned a sassy smile.

"I said make me."

"Oh, Princess, you are a treasure."

Grabbing her hips, he yanked her up, and grasping her firmly at the waist with one hand, he rained a flurry of sharp smacks with the other. Though she squealed and yelped in protest he continued to spank, finally stopping to check her wetness. Finding her soaked, he placed his rigid cock at her entrance and plunged forward. With her cries urging him on, he rode her vigorously, but each time he sensed she was nearing her climax, he slowed to deliver more slaps.

"Sir, please, no more, please," she bleated. "I surrender."

"What does that mean?" he asked, pausing his cock but staying buried inside her.

"Just what I said. I surrender. I won't be a brat."

"Until the next time," he muttered knowingly. "Right?"

"Yes, Sir, but I know what will happen if I am."

"Except I'll make you wait longer, and spank you harder."

"Yes, Sir. I understand. Please let me come?"

Wordlessly clutching her waist, he began to pummel her pussy. With no condom he knew he'd have to withdraw, but he didn't allow the thought to interfere. When she threw back her head and let out her grateful wail, he clenched his teeth and accelerated, using all his self-control to hold his climax at bay, but as her convulsions took hold, her pussy pulsed against his cock. Unable to deny his orgasm he pulled out, and groaning loudly he sprayed his cream across her crimson backside.

As she collapsed on her stomach, though his heart pounded, he made his way to the bathroom, and grabbing a towel he returned to gently wipe her back. Finally dropping next to her, he wrapped her into his arms.

"That was unbelievable," she mumbled. "You're unbelievable. Not even Henry made me feel like this."

Exhausted from the day, and spent from their lovemaking, he knew she was muttering her thoughts as she passed out.

"I know how you feel, Princess," he mumbled, closing his eyes. "I'll see you on the other side."

OFFICER WYATT AND SERGEANT Kelly were driving away from Rise and Shine Stables. Officer Wyatt sat behind the wheel while Sergeant Kelly pondered who to call first. Beside him an evidence bag held a royal blue silk scarf. Claudia Harris had been wearing a royal blue scarf on the night of her disappearance. Sergeant Kelly hadn't found it in the trailer. He'd been chatting to the barn's owner in the tack room when he spotted the dirty, wrinkled scarf lying over a saddle, a saddle that came in with Josh Brady. Not about to leave it behind, the sergeant had dropped it into an evidence bag.

"What do you think about that?" the young officer asked.

"What do I think?" the sergeant repeated. "I think we're about to catch a cowboy."

CHAPTER SEVENTEEN

THERESA WAS STIRRED from a deep sleep by Josh's warm hug, and his cock pushing insistently into her portal. Resting on her side, he had her wrapped up from behind, and as his hands caressed her breasts he pumped with slow, strong strokes. Though still groggy, she surrendered to his ardent skill and rode the gentle waves of pleasure. He carried her from one peak to the next until the last wave crashed on the shore into orgasmic bliss. Again he had pulled out, but with the towel from the evening before lying on top of the bed he didn't have to leave her.

"This is for the birds," he grumbled as he kissed her shoulders. "I've gotta get some condoms."

"But I like you naked."

"There's no gettin' around it until we have some other kinda protection."

"I'll handle it," she promised, rolling over to face him. "When I get back to the ranch I'll call and make an appointment."

"That would make me a very happy cowboy."

"And if you're happy, so am I," she said, then yawning, she closed her eyes and groaned. "I feel like I could sleep for a week."

"I'll bet. I sure would like to stay in bed, but I've gotta check in with everyone then get to Rise and Shine and pack up the trailer."

"What a pain. Do you need Salvo and me to help?"

"No, I'm covered. I have two grooms, and the kids will probably show up. With any luck, by the time I get there the work will be under way."

"Do you know the time?"

"Sure do. I have an internal alarm clock that wakes me up every mornin' at six-thirty."

"Ugh. Anything earlier than seven and I'm a grouch."

"Then I guess you're gonna be a grouch. It's six-forty-five."

"No wonder I'm so tired."

"You go back to sleep. Stay as long as you want. I'll put a Do Not Disturb sign on the door so no-one will knock."

"Perfect. Thank you. Salvo knows if he bothers me I'll cut the curls off that head of hair he's so proud of, but I wish you could stay."

"Don't fret, Princess. We've got plenty of mornin's in our future, but right now I need to get up," he purred. "One instruction. Call me when you get to Dream Horse. I wanna know you're back safe and sound."

"Yes, Sir. Do you know how much I love to say those two words?"

"Probably as much as I love hearin' 'em," he said softly, and giving her a final hug, he slipped out of bed and padded into the bathroom.

Closing her eyes and sighing contentedly, Theresa sank into the mattress and let herself drift away. When she felt his lips on her cheek, she barely managed a mumbled goodbye, and engulfed in a cloud of joy she wandered back into the land of nod.

AT EIGHT-THIRTY WANDA strode into the station.

Two-seconds through the door and her pulse ticked up.

Something was in the air.

That *something* could be anything.

An anonymous tip.

New witness reports.

A likely suspect.

"The chief wants to see you."

Wanda glanced at the officer giving her the message. The frown on his forehead didn't bode well. Prepared for anything, she knocked on the captain's door and poked her head in.

"Hey, Wanda. Come in."

The boss looked none too happy either, but that wasn't unusual.

"You'd better sit down."

"Now I'm getting worried. What's going on, captain?"

"Can't keep a secret in this place. What's that about?"

"Why can't secrets be kept here? Is that what you're asking me?"

"Yeah, I guess I am."

"How many people knew about this alleged secret?"

"Me and a couple of others, plus the two cops who told me."

"Then it's not a secret. Why is everyone looking like someone died? Oh! Sorry. Did someone just die?"

"No, Wanda, but, uh, this is about Josh Brady."

"Josh? Is he okay? He was in Springdale when the twister hit, but I thought he was fine. Did something happen?"

"Something happened, but not what you're thinking. Wanda, I don't know how to tell you this, so I'm just going to say it. Josh is looking like a suspect."

"A suspect? In which case?"

"The guy who drugs the girls and—"

"Stop right there. No way!"

"You must keep an open mind."

"There's an open mind, and then there's a huge gaping hole where no logic or common sense exists."

"Wanda, you need to listen. After you followed Josh back to his house the night Claudia Harris disappeared, did you see him again?"

"No, of course not. He was taking care of the other potential victim."

"No-one saw Claudia either, and you told me yourself, this other girl had also been drugged. Josh has no alibi."

"But—"

"I haven't finished," the captain said, giving her a look that said he was pulling rank.

"Sorry, sir."

"He was the last person to see Claudia that night. I repeat. She wasn't seen again. He's relatively new in the area, and these attacks started a couple of months after he moved here. He studied to be a doctor. He knows medicine. He knows about drugs. How to use them, how much to use, how to best deliver them, all of that. And what better way to keep track of a case, than to become involved."

"He didn't ask to be a part of the investigation. Jack Cooper invited him. You know that. They've been friends for years."

"Doesn't matter. Psychopaths know how to manipulate people. Then we have Claudia Harris showing up in an area where he just happens to be. Springdale."

"This is crazy," Wanda muttered. "None of this proves anything."

"I agree, but something has surfaced that's potentially bad for him. Prepare yourself."

"Go on."

"When that kid found Claudia, one of the responding officers thought it was a bit too coincidental that Josh should be in Springdale at the same time. He decided to stop by the boarding facility where Josh had his horses. He found a dirty blue silk scarf in the barn's tack room sitting on one of his saddles."

Jumping to her feet, Wanda threw her hands in the air and walked around in a circle.

"Wanda? Sit down."

"Has everybody lost their minds?" she exclaimed. "Captain, think about it. A guy who leaves no evidence, zero, nada, zip, not a trace, who's cunning enough to lure these women away from a bar and whisk them off into the night without a soul seeing him, leaves a prime piece of evidence lying around for anyone to see. Not only that, do you honestly think he'd be stupid enough to release a woman in the same area he's going to be in the spotlight for a week? Yeah, sure, that makes sense."

She'd struck a nerve.

A red blush slowly crept up her boss's neck.

"Has anyone bothered showing this scarf to Claudia Harris, or has it already been sent off for analysis?"

"Yeah, the scarf is at the lab. Claudia's pretty out of it, and the powers that be didn't want to wait."

"This is insane. You know that, right?"

"Wanda, we need Josh's DNA."

"Oh, no. Don't look at me to get that for you. Not a chance."

"Just talk to him. Ask him to come in and cooperate."

"Nope. Number one, there's not a chance in hell the scumbag behind these abductions is Josh Brady. Number two, I know how things can go. Some ambitious, idiot detective gets it into his head someone is guilty, and they start looking for things to prove their theory, instead of looking for evidence to find the culprit. You know that better than anyone, and number three, I cannot believe I'm standing here having this conversation with a man I respect and admire. Who are you, and what have you done with the captain."

"Dammit," he grunted, dropping his eyes and staring at the desk.

"Shit! You agree with me!"

"Of course I do," he suddenly shouted. "Don't you think I know all that? Don't you think I've been going through everything you just said over and over in my head a thousand times? Don't you think I made those same arguments to the men sitting behind their big desks with their big fat salaries?"

"I don't understand."

"This case has been dragging on for months, and they want an end to it. This business with Josh is the first scintilla of a lead we've had, and they've pounced all over it."

"What are you saying?"

"I have to follow orders, just like you have to follow orders. If Josh is innocent he has nothing to worry about."

"Captain. You didn't just say that!"

"Our justice system isn't perfect, I grant you that, but it's better than most, and more importantly, it's the only one we have."

"Those are just words, and there is no way I'm going to let a good man—no—a great man, a caring man, a man who has given up all his free time to try to catch this asshole—there is no way I'm going to let him get railroaded."

"Wanda—"

"No!" she exclaimed, raising her hand. "Now you have to listen to me."

"Go on."

"Neither are you!"

TO JOSH'S RELIEF NO-one in his group had been injured, but when he arrived at the barn, Smitty, the manager, asked him into his office for a private word.

"I don't know what's goin' on," Smitty began, "but I gotta real bad feelin'. Last night, kinda late, two policemen arrived here askin' questions."

"Questions about what? You look so worried."

"I reckon I am, but not for me, for you. They asked how well I knew you, if I'd ever seen you rattled, stuff like that, then they picked up a blue scarf that was sittin' on one of your saddles. They dropped it into a bag and left."

"That's weird."

"They were real interested in that scarf, Josh."

"If you're askin' me where it came from, I found it on the floor of the trailer when I was unloadin' the tack. All the kids had gone into town and I didn't know who it belonged to, so I left it on a saddle. I figured someone would claim it."

"Well, the police have it now."

"I can't imagine why, but thanks for the heads up. I'm sure it's nothing. Maybe someone lost one of those crazy expensive scarves and they thought they'd found it, though why they'd think I'd be interested in a woman's scarf is beyond me. I'm sure I'll be able to clear it up when they get in touch, assuming they do."

But as he and his group packed up the trailer and headed home, he couldn't shake the unsettling news. When he pulled into Tall Tree Farms, he was grateful to be back, and after unloading the horses and making sure they were safely in their paddocks, he hurried across to see Queenie. The big chestnut mare was standing in her shelter, her breakfast in front of her untouched.

"What's the matter girl?" he muttered, quickly opening the gate and walking over to her. "Hey, aren't you feelin' good?"

Raising her head, she gazed at him, her big brown eyes reaching through his chest and touching his heart.

"Hey, big girl, I'm fine. The tornado didn't come near me. It was miles away."

But his reassuring words had no impact.

"Okay, yeah, there's a problem. I don't know what's goin' on just yet, but I'll take care of whatever it is."

To his great relief, she let out a snort, then shook her body the way she would after rolling in the dirt.

"What are you doin', girl? Shakin' off the bad energy?"

Dropping her head into his chest, she gently nudged him, and for a brief moment Josh felt the threat of tears.

"Dang it, Queenie, how do you know so much?" he murmured, wrapping his arms around her neck. "I sure wish you could talk. I've gotta feelin' you know more than I do."

Snorting again, she lifted her head and stared at him.

"Trust me. I'll sort it out. Would you please eat your breakfast? I don't need to be worryin' about you as well."

She held his gaze for a minute, then ambled to her hay and began to munch. Relieved to see her eating, he moved through the gate and started back to the barn.

"Okay. Somethin's goin' down. She knows it, and sooner or later I guess I will too," he muttered, but just as he finished speaking his phone rang. Pulling it from his pocket he glanced at the screen. Wanda. "Huh. Looks like it's gonna be sooner."

CHAPTER EIGHTEEN

AS WANDA OUTLINED THE information about the scarf, Josh hurried though the barn and into his office. Closing the door, he began to pace as she reported her concerns. Though questions came to mind he held his tongue. During his training as a doctor he'd learn to pay attention. Any queries followed, then armed with all available information a diagnosis could be made. An excellent listener, he also possessed an analytical mind.

"That's where we are," Wanda finished. "You're now a blip on the radar screen. Regardless of the results from forensics, probably before they're even known, you'll be getting a visit from the detectives in charge of the case. As you know the first few victims were in Marionville and that's where they're based. Josh, are you there?"

"Yeah."

The deeply disturbing news had set his brain spinning. When he'd returned to Rise and Shine that morning, many of the saddles had already been loaded into the trailer, and he hadn't given the scarf a second thought.

"Wanda, I think that scarf is gonna prove significant."

"Why do you say that?"

"I could be wrong, but I'm familiar with the show clothes my juniors wear, and the amateurs too, though I only have a couple of adults. Two of the mothers to be precise. I don't recall any of them wearin' a scarf like that, and certainly not that size. They wear kerchiefs around their necks, not shawls around their shoulders. I remember wonderin' what it was doin' there when I found it. The tack compartment in the trailer doesn't have much space. It's organized and kept clean. The scarf was filthy and wrinkled. Looks like whoever is behind the abductions has decided I'm gonna be the scapegoat."

"I'm sorry to say I've already come to that conclusion," Wanda said solemnly, "but I wanted to hear your take."

"How the hell do I handle this, Wanda?"

"Let's start with the visit from the detectives. For the moment you need to avoid them. Keep your eyes open, and if you see an unfamiliar car driving into Tall Tree Farms, jump on that amazing horse you're always telling me about and hit the trail. If you hear a car pull outside your house and you're not expecting anyone, duck out the back."

"But I haven't done anything. Won't that make me look guilty?"

"Not initially. They'll just think they've missed you. We can spend ages trying to catch up with someone. It happens all the time."

"Uh, Wanda, you shouldn't be tellin' me any of this. I appreciate it more than I can say, but I don't want you stickin' your neck out. You could lose your job."

"Josh, this is a no-brainer. I don't want to see you go down for a heinous crime you didn't commit, while the guilty bastard disappears and hurts other women somewhere else."

"I'm at a loss for words."

"I'm sure you are. This is a shock. I was shocked when my captain laid all this out, but forewarned is forearmed. You need to keep your head, and do your best not to change your habits or walk around looking worried."

"Thanks. I can see why that would look bad, but it wouldn't have occurred to me."

"Getting back to the detectives. I'm hoping we'll have all this figured out before they catch up with you, but if we don't, and you find yourself being peppered with questions, first rule that cannot be broken, answer truthfully. Even if you think your answer won't help you, tell the truth. Oftentimes we'll ask questions we already know the answer to, and if we hear a lie, it only serves to confirm our suspicions. Besides that, lying to the police is a crime."

"This is beyond anything I've ever faced," Josh said grimly. "I already feel outta my depth."

"I understand, but you're a smart guy and I know you're Mr. Cool under pressure. If you end up being interrogated don't let them rattle you. Stay calm, and don't be defensive. If you feel they're overstepping or trying to trap you, stop, take a breath, and tell them the crime they're investigating is deadly serious, you take it seriously, and you don't want to answer any more questions without legal counsel. Smart people do that. It doesn't point to guilt."

"Damn."

"Do you know a good criminal defense lawyer?"

"I know a dozen medical malpractice attorneys."

"Get a referral. If you need to make that phone call you won't be scrambling."

"Wanda, this is crazy."

"Yeah, but being prepared will go a long way if things come down to the wire, though I'm hoping it won't come to that. My gut tells me leaving that scarf is his first mistake."

"What makes you say that?"

"Why now? Is he getting nervous? More importantly, he's set us in motion, and because he has I'm throwing the book out the window. Playing by the rules won't work when there are ambitious detectives looking for an arrest, especially when they're supported by the higher-ups. Don't get me wrong. Most of the people I've worked with are decent, but this case has been dragging on for too long. Everyone is anxious. That's when mistakes are made and people's logic can get twisted.

"I'm sure glad you're on my side, Wanda."

"I am, and I'm on the side of all the women this creep has harmed. So, cowboy, it's time to get to work. We need to do what we discussed last night. Can you meet me at the The Horseshoe Tavern in an hour?"

"Sure, no problem."

"I know I've thrown a bunch of stuff at you, but you can handle it. The good news is we have some breathing space. We won't get any results back from forensics for several days. And you'll be in for a surprise when I see you."

"I'm not sure I can handle any more surprises."

"You'll love this one. I'd tell you what it is, but even though I'm on a burner phone I still don't want to mention it. Oh, one more thing. Think about who knew you were heading up to Springdale, and who had access to your trailer."

"Hells bells, Wanda. I don't need to think about that. Everyone knew I was goin' to that show, just like all the trainers around here. As far as the trailer is concerned, anyone could've come in here and left that damn scarf. The owners live on the property, but the house is up the hill and I don't think Ben and Jerry would sound the alarm if someone sneaked in here in the middle of the night. Maybe if they were haulin' a trailer and makin' a bunch of noise, but on foot? I doubt it."

"Who are Ben and Jerry?"

"Two golden retrievers. They belong to the owners."

"Cute."

"Yeah, they are. Rascals, both of 'em, but they're good boys. Nice to think about them at a time like this. Normalcy."

"You need to keep thoughts like that in abundance. They'll help you stay grounded. The last thing you want to do is panic."

"Don't worry. That's not gonna happen. I don't panic easy. Just the opposite. That's one thing a doctor and a horse trainer have in common. They have to stay calm when things start goin' wrong."

"Ah. I see your point. I need to go. I'll see you at the tavern, oh, and park somewhere outta sight."

"Wow. I thought that twister was about the most dangerous thing I'd be facin' for a while, but it doesn't compare to this."

"Hopefully it's one that'll be over just as fast."

"From your lips, Wanda. From your lips."

Ending the call, Josh dropped on the couch and replayed the conversation in his head. Processing the information calmed him, and he came out of his reverie with a sense of clarity, and also a belief the man behind the abductions was local. Someone who knew Josh, where he worked, and that he would be taking his trailer to Springdale. Last and most importantly, the man had been at the Horseshoe Tavern the night he'd taken Theresa home.

Because of his attraction to Theresa he'd been keeping a close eye on her, and thinking back to that night, he didn't recall any men sidling up to her. He also remembered not being surprised. Most of the women were laughing and drinking, but Theresa had been sitting at the bar with a cool demeanor, wearing clothes that didn't fit the scene.

"As much as I wanted to, even I didn't feel comfortable goin' up to her," he muttered, "so who the hell got close enough to slip somethin' in her drink? Dammit. It had to be the bartender. Duke Palmer!"

The ringing of his phone made him jump. In spite of the thundercloud hanging over him, when he saw Theresa's name on the screen he broke into a smile.

"Hey, Princess."

"Hi, Josh. Is this a bad time?"

"Nope. Your timin' is perfect. I needed a distraction. What's goin' on?"

"Just following orders. I'm checking in to let you know I'm back."

"Good girl. You'll get a big hug when I see you."

"How was your trip to Tall Tree? Did you take the main road?"

"Yep. I don't like haulin' through the back country. If anything happens there's no-one around to help, and sometimes cell phone reception can be dicey."

"Good point. Josh, can I swing by and visit Queenie later this morning?"

"You can swing by and visit Queenie any time. I know she'd love to see you."

"Wonderful. Thank you."

"What time are you thinkin'?"

"I'll probably leave here in about an hour. Things are quiet for me right now. I still have work to do, but I'm not in the mood and I can get it done this afternoon. I don't need to be back here until noonish. I won't have a whole lot of time, but I'll be able to spend thirty-minutes or so."

"I may not be here, but feel free to take her out for a walk. Would you feel comfortable doin' that?"

"If you think I can, then sure."

"There are plenty of people around, and Sam will be cleanin' up after the storm if you need him, but I'm not worried. Queenie loves you. She'll be a perfect lady. Her halter is on the stand by her paddock."

"I remember. This is fantastic. Thanks so much."

"You're welcome, but I should be thankin' you. Don't forget to take her some treats. She'll be expectin' them."

"Wouldn't dream of it. Josh, I'm hearing something in your voice, like you're distracted, or worried. Is everything okay?"

He paused. He didn't want to lie to her.

"Whatta you mean, Princess?"

"I'm not sure. You'd tell me if there was something wrong, wouldn't you?"

"Am I that transparent?"

"Uh, I don't know. Whatever I'm picking up wasn't obvious. More like a feeling."

"Damn. You and Queenie. You're both scary."

"Does that mean I'm right?"

"I got some disturbin' news, but I'd rather not discuss it on the phone. When we meet up I'll fill you in."

"Are you okay?"

"Yeah, I'm fine, but like I said, I can't talk about it right now. Are you doin' anything later?"

"I'm glad you asked. Heath and Carly want to have you over for dinner tonight. Can you make it?"

"I sure can, and I'd really like that. It's about time I met them."

"Great. Is six o'clock okay?"

"You bet. I'm lookin' forward to it, and thank them for the invitation."

"Sure will. I told them everything, and they want to thank you personally for getting me out of The Horseshoe that night."

"I'm just glad I was there. I'd better get movin', Princess. There's somewhere I need to be."

"Sure, of course. If I miss you this morning, I'll see you tonight. Bye, Josh. Take care."

"Bye, Princess."

Ending the call, Josh glanced at his watch. If he left for the tavern he'd get there before Wanda and the idea appealed to him. He could have a quiet poke around by himself. Not wanting to get held up, he decided to slip away quietly. Though his truck was still hooked up to the trailer, his Jeep Cherokee was in the guest parking area. Hoping not to run into any clients, he moved quickly from his office, marched past the trailer, and turned down the front side of the barn. There were several cars near his, but no people. Hastily marching forward, he climbed behind the wheel and headed off.

CHAPTER NINETEEN

THE HORSESHOE TAVERN sat near a lake at the end of a one lane gravel road lined by trees. Exiting the main road, Josh drove his jeep down the paved street that led to the turnoff. The area was ranch land. Homes were spread by acreage, cattle languidly grazed next to their equine neighbors in separate paddocks. The rural scene promised peace and tranquility, never suggesting a madman could be lurking in the shadows. Passing only one car, Josh had no fears that he'd been followed, though from everything Wanda had said he wouldn't be surprised if the police decided to place him under surveillance. Even with skimpy evidence, Josh had no doubt they were excited to have a suspect.

As he neared the tavern, he searched for an area in the trees wide enough to accommodate the jeep, and though he spotted several, the car would still be visible. The pub came into view, and with the lake on the right, and what appeared to be dense forest to the left, his only option was to drive to the rear of the structure. Moving slowly past the parking area he glanced back into the woods, and to his surprise he spied an opening. Rolling to a stop he lowered his window and craned his neck.

"Look at that," he muttered. "I'd call that an area worth explorin.'"

The angle at which the trees had been cleared made it virtually invisible unless you were viewing it from behind the tavern. Slowly making a U-turn, he drove cautiously into the heavily wooded thicket. The rough trail offered barely enough room between the trees for his jeep, but in a matter of seconds he found himself in an area large enough to turn his jeep around and drive out. Pulling to a stop, he stepped out and stared at the clearing in wonder. Felling the trees and removing the stumps would have taken a great deal of work, then sending his eyes in the direction of the tavern, he discovered it was clearly visible through the trees.

"Someone went to a shitload of trouble to make this place, and it was all about watchin' the bar and the parkin' lot."

Working with Wanda had taught him a few things, and in spite of the recent storm, lowering his gaze he studied the ground looking for evidence of an observer. Leaves and brambles covered the forest floor, and finding a long, thin stick, walking at a snail's pace towards the tavern, he moved the debris aside. When he neared the last line of trees he let out a disappointed sigh, but lifting his eyes he discovered he had an elevated, unobstructed view of the building and surrounding area. Then it hit him. At night, dressed in dark clothing, he'd be invisible. Tossing the stick aside and dropping to his knees, Josh moved the leaves from side to side.

He caught his breath.

An empty cigarette pack.

Then he found the butts.

He'd hit an evidence gold mine.

Hearing an approaching vehicle he looked towards the gravel lane. A black sedan with tinted windows and government issued license plates told him it was probably Wanda, but wanting to be sure before revealing himself he waited until the car rolled to a stop in the parking lot. To his surprise, a tall man with crew cut and a marine's physique stepped from the driver's seat. Thinking he must be one of the detectives, Josh ducked behind a tree, but a moment later Wanda appeared from the passenger's side. Relieved, he stepped out and made his way down the low bank and jogged towards them.

"Hey, Wanda."

Turning around, Wanda waved, but the man swiveled. Josh smiled. Mr. Crewcut had been trained.

"Hi, Josh. This is my Captain. Captain Lewis, this is Josh Brady."

"An honor to finally meet you, Captain," Josh said, extending his hand. "Thanks so much for allowing me to work with Wanda. It's been fascinatin.'"

"She spoke highly of you, but I didn't okay anything. If she wants a male friend by her side when she's out for a drink, that's up to her."

"Ah, right. I understand, sir," Josh said knowingly, then looking at him intently, he added, "Captain, I think I just stumbled into something important."

"And what would that be, son?"

"Behind those trees is a clearing, and you can't see the entrance unless you drive past it and look back. It's obviously manmade, and it's the perfect observation point for the tavern and this parking area."

"Huh. That is interesting."

"There's more. I found an empty cigarette pack and some butts by those trees. It's a perfect lookout point."

"Did you touch them?" the captain asked briskly.

"No, sir."

"You did good! Would you two excuse me? I need to take a leak, and it seems like those woods over there would be the perfect place. Wanda, take your side-kick and look for signs of that break-in."

"There was a break-in?" Josh asked. "When?"

"I'll leave you to fill him in, Wanda," the captain declared. "I'll be back in a few minutes."

"Come on, Josh," Wanda said with a warm smile, clearly delighted by Josh's find, "let's take a look around the back."

"What's goin' on? Why is the captain here?" Josh asked in a hushed whisper as he joined her.

"He wants to save your bacon just as much as I do."

"You're kiddin'? How did that happen?"

"Once he realized leaving an incriminating scarf sitting on one of your saddles made absolutely no sense, he had to admit you couldn't possibly be that stupid. The funny thing is, when I thought about it, if you were the perp, putting it there would have been a stroke of genius."

"I'm confused. Why would that have made me a genius?"

"Obviously you wouldn't if you were the guilty party."

"Oh! Like a double bluff. See? I just don't have a duplicitous mind."

"Exactly. Well, here we are. The back of the tavern."

"What's this about a break-in?"

"That's what the captain will say if anyone drives up, and it will also explain our presence if I have to write a report. We received an anonymous tip."

"Why would a captain respond to a break-in? Isn't that below his pay grade?"

"For sure, but we happened to be close by when the call came and he decided to take it."

"You mean, a call actually did come in?"

"Of course. How could we respond to a call if it didn't come in? Anymore questions?"

"I'm speechless, so no, except where do we go from here?"

"I'd like to get inside and take a look around, but I'll have to kick the door in."

"You can do that?"

"If I have to, and it looks that way."

"You're actually gonna boot that door open?"

"Not until you step back."

"Be careful."

"Nothing to it."

"Is this far enough?"

"Looks good. Do you see any cameras?"

"Uh, nope. None above the door or the posts."

"I'm not surprised. If he doesn't have them inside the tavern, he's not likely to have them out here."

Suddenly, and with lightning speed, Wanda swung her body sideways to the door, lifted her leg, and slammed her foot against the wood just above the lock.

"Damn," Josh muttered as the door burst open. "That's impressive, like, seriously."

"Like I said, nothing to it," she quipped. "Make sure you don't touch anything, and I mean anything. In fact, here," she said, reaching into her pocket and handing him a pair of latex gloves.

Stepping inside, the only light came from the open door, and pausing, Wanda raised her hand.

"Stop. It's easy to trip over something in a situation like this."

"How do we turn on the lights?"

"Your body is blocking the doorway. If you take a cautious step to the side, I should be able to see the switch. If I can't I'll use my flashlight. Thank you. Yep, there it is!"

Stepping to the wall next to the door frame, she flipped the knob and the room came into view. A small desk and chair sat in a corner, various supplies on shelving, a filing cabinet, and crates of beer and wine were stacked against a wall. The concrete floor sported a worn rug, and moving it with her foot, Wanda found nothing suspicious underneath.

"No trap doors here. This is solid."

"Anything?" the captain asked as he strode in, his head barely missing the top of the door frame.

"Nothing looks out of order, sir," Wanda replied. "We're about to go into the bar area."

"I'll mosey around here and see if the intruder left any trace. Whoever it was had one heck of a kick."

"You can say that again," Josh remarked with a grin. "I wouldn't like to be on the receivin' end of it, that's for sure."

The captain looked at him stone-faced.

"I didn't mean to say anything out of turn," Josh added hastily.

"Just breaking your balls, son," said the beefy man with a chuckle. "Can't help myself sometimes. Go and keep Wanda company, and check the facilities. Amazin' what people stash behind the towel dispensers."

"Really?"

"Nah, just doing it again, but check anyway. You never know."

Not quite sure what to make of him, and feeling unnerved, Josh hurried into the tavern. The bar stools were sitting on top of the counter, and Wanda was on her hands and knees studying the floor.

"What are you searchin' for?"

"I noticed this wire," she replied without looking up, "but now I realize it's not a wire, it's a cable."

"A cable? Must be for the television set."

"No. The TV is above the bar and you can see where the cables and wiring go through a hole into the back room. This is something else."

"But he doesn't have cameras in here."

"So he claims. I'm going to follow it and find out exactly where it leads and what it's for. You trace it back the other way."

"I can already tell you the cable leads behind the bar," he replied, carefully lifting the hinged panel and surveying the shelves under the counter. "There's some kind of black box here, and that's plugged into an outlet. Maybe a nanny cam?"

"Possibly, but this cable is going into the hallway that leads to the exit. Come with me, Josh."

"I don't know much about this stuff, but can't you get equipment that's wireless? Why go to all this trouble?"

"That technology probably wasn't available when he put this in, or it was very expensive. This is crazy. Am I nuts, or is it feeding back into the room behind the bar?"

"Sure looks like it, but why bring it all the way around here? Why not just thread it through the wall underneath the television?"

"Good question, and there has to be a camera in there," Wanda said grimly. "I sure hope it's not aimed at the door I kicked in."

"Damn."

Walking swiftly back to the room, they searched along the baseboard for the cable, but found nothing.

"I don't understand," Wanda declared. "What the hell? Any ideas?"

"None. I wonder if it's an old antenna of some kind that goes up to the roof, and he just never bothered taking it out."

"Then what's the box under the counter for?"

"Oh, yeah. Good question. Where did your captain go?"

"He'll be poking around outside, but mostly keeping watch in case Derrick Palmer shows up."

"Can I ask you something?"

"Of course."

"Why is he doing this? You said he's by the book. I find it hard to believe he's goin' out on a limb like this because he thinks I'm innocent and he wants to catch the bad guy."

"Um, well..."

"Wanda! What aren't you tellin' me?"

"I'll tell you if you swear you'll keep it to yourself."

"Sure. I swear I won't breathe a word."

"He does believe you're in danger of being falsely accused, but he's also supporting me because he and my dad are really close. They met when they were in the marines. When they served in Iraq my dad saved his life."

"What?"

"Yeah. Pretty heavy. When dad found out who my new captain was, you can imagine how excited he was. The station is aware my dad and the captain know each other, but that's it. It would make the situation difficult for us both if anyone found out."

"Wow. I'm feelin' pretty blessed right now. Thanks for tellin' me."

"When I have to, I can talk to him like I can talk to my dad and he doesn't take offense. In fact, he says when I go to the mat for something I remind him of how my dad used to be when he'd get worked up."

"I promise not to tell a soul."

"Thanks, Josh. Now I need to make sure that cable isn't attached to anything in this room. I can't leave until we do."

"Then let's get to it."

For twenty minutes they searched everywhere except behind the bottles of beer and wine. The crates weren't just heavy, they were solid and pressed up against the wall. Even if the cable exited behind them it couldn't have been attached to anything, and they scrutinized the front of the boxes to make sure one of them wasn't hiding a camera. Finally giving up, they walked outside to meet up with the captain, but he was wandering around the slope that led down to the lake.

"Wait for me by the car," Wanda said as she headed off to speak with him. "I won't be long."

"Hey, Wanda, it wasn't a total bust. I found that cigarette package."

"I don't know what you're talking about," she said with a wink, then turned and walked away.

Leaning against the black sedan, Josh's analytical mind clicked in. There was something bothering him about the room, but he couldn't put his finger on it. When his phone rang he welcomed the distraction, and looking at the screen he broke into a smile.

"Theresa, your timin' is perfect. Are you with Queenie?"

"I am, she's wonderful, but we have a problem."

"You and Queenie?"

"The thing is, I took her out of her paddock for a walk, and she literally dragged me over to a trailer. Sam told me it's your two-horse."

"That darn mare. She wants to go on a trail ride off the property."

"But, Josh, you don't understand. She won't leave. No-one can get her to move."

"You're kiddin'?"

"I need to tell you something," she said suddenly whispering, "but I don't want anyone to hear and I don't want to leave her."

"Text me."

"Okay."

Ending the call, he waited anxiously. Seconds later her message landed.

She doesn't want to be here. You need to come back and take her out. I can call Heath and ask if she can stay at Dream Horse Ranch for a couple of days. I'm sure he won't mind. Do you want me to, or do you think I'm being an idiot?

A cold chill pricked his skin.

Yes, call him. I'm on my way. Don't tell anyone I'm taking her there.

CHAPTER TWENTY

THE MOMENT JOSH LOWERED the ramp, Queenie marched into the trailer, then snorting loudly, she dove into the hay in the feed compartment.

"I noticed she'd barely touched her breakfast," Theresa remarked as Josh closed up the back doors. "I didn't know what to think. Now I understand."

"Yeah, I know. She was upset when I got here, but I thought she'd settled."

"Where are you off to?" Sam asked, ambling up to join them.

"Not sure. I'd like to show Theresa the trail by the falls, but I haven't made up my mind. The rain may have made it too muddy."

"Have fun. What time do you think you'll be back?"

"I've got nothin' much happenin' today," Josh said vaguely, "and you know how trail ridin' can be. I'll see you when I see you. I hope the cleanin' up goes quick."

"I could use another hand."

"Sorry," Josh said with a grin. "I've got two females with me. My hands are full."

Chuckling, Sam shook his head and walked away.

"Okay, Princess, let's get this unhappy horse outta here."

"What do you think the problem is?"

"I have no idea, but I've learned to listen. She's never been wrong. You'd better drive in front of me. You'll need to lead me in when we get to the ranch. I won't know where to go."

"Will do."

Pecking him on the cheek, she hurried to the Land Rover, climbed in and started down the driveway, stopping at the end to wait for Josh to catch up. It was then she remembered Duke Palmer's horse was also at Heath's. Jumping from the SUV, she trotted up to meet Josh's truck.

"Hey, what's up?" Josh asked, lowering his window.

"I just remembered something. Duke Palmer's horse is there. He dropped him off a couple of days ago. I don't suppose it matters, but I had this feeling I should mention it."

"Is Heath a good friend of his?"

"I don't know if they're good friends or just know each other. Apparently when Duke goes on one of his micro-brewery hunts he boards his gelding at the ranch."

"Do you know when he's comin' back?"

"I think he's gone for a week, but I don't know if that means five days or seven days. Is it important?"

"I'll explain when we have a minute. Thanks for the heads-up."

As Theresa walked back to the Land Rover, Josh pondered the news. Though he had no intention of discussing the morning's events with Heath and Carly Boyd, if the conversation turned to what happened to Theresa, or the disappearance of Claudia Harris from The Horseshoe Tavern, he'd have to be careful. Heath and Duke could be buddies.

But Josh was also concerned about his mare.

"Why were you so hellbent on gettin' outta Tall Tree Farms?" he mumbled to himself as they rolled on to the street. "I sure hope I find out soon. We can't stay away forever."

His head spinning with thoughts of Duke Palmer, the scarf, and Queenie's odd behavior, the twenty-minute drive flew by, and following Theresa through the gates of Dream Horse Ranch, he let out a low whistle. An impressive house sat atop a knoll overlooking the outdoor riding ring, three quaint cottages and the paddocks beyond. The indoor arena adjacent to a picturesque red and white barn, sported fabric side panels that had been lowered due to the inclement weather, and though storm debris still littered the grounds, the property was beautifully landscaped and immaculately maintained. Driving past the house and approaching the parking area, he smiled. It offered plenty of room to unload safely. As they rolled to a stop, an attractive young woman moved slowly out of the barn and moved towards the truck.

"Hi, I'm Carly," she said as Josh stepped out. "Very nice to meet you."

"Hey, Carly. I really appreciate this, especially with no notice."

"After what you did for Theresa, boarding your horse is the least we can do."

"Forgive me for askin', but are you okay? You're movin' like you're hurtin'?"

"I was bucked off the other day. I didn't come out of it real well."

"Oh, that's right. Chuck."

"Yeah, Chuck, and I have to thank you a second time for the solution to his problem. I just wish I'd met you before I got on."

"Me too. Sorry you're still sore."

"I'm healing fast. I'll be fine in a couple of days. Let's get your mare out. Hi, Theresa."

"Hi, Carly," Theresa said with a smile as she joined them. "Thanks so much. Where are Andy and Salvo?"

"They had to drive out to the back pastures to check on the fencing after the storm," Carly replied as Josh lowered the ramp.

"Will they be back for lunch?"

"I doubt it, but that picnic hamper you took to Springdale was still in the truck." Then turning to look at Queenie, she broke into a wide smile. "Josh, what a gorgeous mare," she exclaimed, stepping forward and stroking the horse's neck. "May I give her a carrot? I brought one out with me, and look, she's already sniffing around my pocket."

"She's pretty smart."

"No kidding," Carly said with a laugh as she held the carrot and watched Queenie happily gobble it up. "I can see why you fell in love, Theresa. She's so sweet."

"The sweetest," Theresa murmured, circling her arms around Queenie's neck and hugging her.

"There's a stall ready, but she can go into a paddock if you want," Carly offered. "The one we have available is on the small side, but it's also the closest to the barn."

"She'd love that. Thanks. Theresa, would you like to take her down?"

"I sure would," she replied eagerly, taking the lead rope. "Come on, Queenie. Let me show you your hotel room."

As she began walking towards the pasture, Queenie lifted her nose in the air and let out a whinny.

"Announcing her arrival," Josh remarked as he closed up the trailer.

"I'm amazed that Theresa has no fear. Before she met your horse she couldn't even bring herself to open her hand and offer treats. And I can't believe she actually sat on her."

"Yep. Her choice. I had nothin' to do with it. She and Queenie had an immediate connection. I've seen it happen before, but not like that."

"Josh, can you stick around for lunch? I know Heath would love to meet you. He's tied up in his office right now, but the invitation comes from us both."

"That's mighty kind of you. Thanks. I'd like that."

"You can unhook your trailer and leave it here if you want. We have plenty of room."

"Maybe I will. I won't be needin' it."

"Josh, can I ask why you needed to move your horse? It doesn't matter, and you don't have to tell me, but I am curious."

"I'm sure I'm not tellin' you anything you don't know when I say a horse needs a change of scenery now and then, just like we do."

"Yep, they do. Heath and I often load up and go on a trail ride somewhere new. It's great for all our heads, and look at her. She's having a ball."

"Oh, no."

Finding the muddiest patch in the paddock, Queenie was happily rolling.

"I know what I'll be doing later this afternoon," Josh said with a chuckle. "I also know what comes next. And there she goes!"

Getting to her feet, Queenie shook, then bolted, and began galloping around the field, tossing her head, whinnying loudly, and bucking like a bronc.

"She's contagious," Carly declared, laughing out loud as the horses in the adjacent fields decided to join the fun and kick up their heels.

"Queenie's started a party," Theresa exclaimed, striding up to join them. "I knew she'd be happy here."

"She's welcome to stay as long as you need her to," Carly said happily. "I'm going to love having her around."

"It should only be for a couple of days."

"I'm sorry, but I need to get up to the house," Theresa said, glancing at her watch. "I need to get lunch on. Any special requests, Carly?"

"Can you make your chicken burgers?"

"Sure. I haven't served those in over a month. Great suggestion. What about you, Josh?"

"Whatever's comin' off the grill."

"Josh, come into the barn and I'll show you where everything is," Carly suggested. "I apologize in advance for moving slowly."

"Sounds good, and no apology needed."

"See you up at the house," Theresa said, heading towards the Land Rover. "Figure thirty-minutes."

As she drove away, Carly walked Josh down to the barn, and entering the airy, light barn he nodded approvingly.

"Love how wide the aisle is. This is a beautiful facility."

"Heath built this place and he'd love to hear that. Getting where he is now hasn't been easy."

"The journey rarely is, but that's what makes the success so gratifyin'. Excuse me, that's my phone," he declared, but pulling it from his pocket and seeing Sam's name, he ignored the call. "Nothin' that can't wait," he said with a grin, stuffing it back in his pocket. "Show me what's what."

IN THE PARKING AREA of Tall Tree Farms, wearing grim frowns Detectives Jack Collins and Steve Yates leaned against their navy blue Dodge Charger Pursuit. Though unmarked, the spotlights near the side mirrors, the license plates and three additional antennas on the car's roof advertised its use as a police vehicle.

"Fucking annoying," Jack grunted. "Why the hell did that barn manager tell us Brady would be here all day?"

"Take it easy, Steve. The cowboy loaded his horse and went out on a trail ride. The manager couldn't have known he'd do that, and you're the one who insisted we had to keep our arrival under wraps."

"You agreed!"

"Yeah, well, you're like my wife. There are times it's just easier to say yes."

"What do you make of this place?" Jack asked, changing the subject. "Captain Lewis didn't seem particularly interested in Brady. I don't get it. He's our only suspect, and we're damn lucky to finally have one."

"Must have something to do with that break-in at the tavern. Whatever he found was enough to get a forensics unit out there. Weird, though, that a Captain decided to answer that call."

"He was down the street when the call came in. There's nothing weird about that," Jack argued. "Besides, it seems likely the last victim's abduction probably happened there. He's probably playing catch up. That whole area should have been taped off way before now."

"That's a bit harsh. Her husband didn't report her gone until yesterday, and they had to check out a few things before they could make it an official missing persons case. By that time the storm had rolled in."

"I still think he waited too long, and need I remind you, Josh Brady was the last person she was seen with in that parking lot."

"Doesn't mean anything."

"The hell it doesn't."

"Not in the scheme of things," Steve said with a sigh. "So, back to the point. Do we wait around here until our cowboy gets back? How long do trail rides last?"

"I have no idea. I've never sat on a horse in my life," Jack muttered. "I still think we should poke around his office."

"As I said before, no warrant."

"Not his property."

"Again, as I said before, that's debatable. He leases that barn, including that office. The barn manager doesn't have the authority to permit a search. The owners, maybe, but not that pinhead barn manager."

"But—"

"Jack! Give it up. You're not winning this one. As far as this place goes, anyone could wander in here and plant that scarf in Brady's trailer, and if the test results show it was the victim's, why would a guilty guy leave it sitting out in plain sight for someone to find? I don't like the way this smells. You know what else? I'm betting Tom Lewis has come to the same conclusion."

"Think what you want, Brady is still my prime suspect."

"Then you should make sure anything we find can't be thrown out by some smart-ass lawyer."

"True."

"Thank you. Now, back to the point. Do we sit here and wait, or try again tomorrow? I vote for a run over to the tavern, then swinging by the station and checking in with Lewis. Or the other way around."

"Let's do Lewis first," Jack suggested. "There might be more to learn at the crime scene if we give it another hour. Do you mind driving?"

"No problem."

Climbing into the charger, they moved down the driveway, then sped away. Watching from the barn, Sam shook his head.

"Dumb city slickers," he grunted. "I swear, my Ben and Jerry have more brains than those two."

CHAPTER TWENTY-ONE

RETRIEVING A KEY TAPED to the bottom of his desk lamp, Captain Tom Lewis unlocked the bottom drawer and smiled at his prized collection. A bottle of one-hundred year-old Scotch Whiskey and crystal tumbler, sat next to a humidor holding a dozen illegally imported Cuban cigars. Behind them a modest orange box contained a collection of chocolates from one of the world's finest chocolatiers. Galler. He ordered them from Belgium twice a year. Impossible to eat only one, he limited himself to no more than three on the day he indulged.

He only enjoyed the delectable chocolates, the smooth whiskey, and the fine cigar to celebrate a triumph.

Carefully lifting out the bottle and crystal tumbler, he poured himself a generous amount, then placed the glass in front of the antique inkwell his wife had given him for their thirty-fifth wedding anniversary. A cigar followed, then bringing out the orange box, he lifted the lid and inhaled the rich sweet aroma. Studying the selection, he chose three, and placed them next to the cigar. Satisfied, he returned the bottle and the box, closed the drawer, locked it, and put the key back under the lamp.

He smiled.

He'd solved the puzzle.

Certain pieces were missing, but they'd show up.

They always did.

But a knock on his door interrupted his reverie.

"You wanted to see me, Captain?"

"Wanda, come in."

"Captain!" she exclaimed, staring at the items perfectly lined up and waiting to be relished. "You know!"

"I believe I do. Did you manage to reach Derrick Palmer and tell him about the break-in?"

"Yes, sir. We had his cell phone number on file in case of an emergency. It was him, right? Derrick's the dirtbag?"

"No comment. Tell me about the conversation."

"There's not much to tell. He was alarmed, of course, asked if any of his stock had been taken, then said he'd be back tomorrow."

"You didn't mention the clearing in the woods?"

"No, sir. I kept it to myself just as you asked. I told him we believed the tavern was the site of an abduction. He took that in stride until I informed him his property was now being treated as a crime scene and a forensics team was there."

"Uh-huh. What else?"

"He asked when he could reopen. I told him I wasn't sure."

"Did you run a check on the property?"

"I contacted the title company and they'll be sending over the report later today."

"Good. Excuse me," he said as his desk phone buzzed. "Yes, Millie, what is it? They are? Fine, send them in. Our intrepid detectives have arrived," he declared, hanging up the receiver.

"Should I leave?"

"Hell no, you'll enjoy this. Take that chair by the window and watch. Here's a pad and pen. Act like you're making notes."

"Captain Lewis, Detective Steve Yates and Detective Jack Collins," his secretary declared, ushering them in as Wanda moved quickly to sit down.

"Hello, gentlemen. Have a seat. Steve Yates, we've crossed paths."

"Briefly at the award ceremony when you were awarded the Medal Of Valor."

"I'd love to hear your story, captain," Jack said. "All I know is you walked into a drug den and saved two guys working undercover. I heard there were a dozen bad asses with guns and somehow you got the better of them."

"A dozen?" Tom repeated with a frown. "That's what you heard?"

"Yeah, I figured a dozen was probably an exaggeration," Jack said with a chuckle. "How many were there?"

"Bad-asses? Seventeen, and two Rottweilers."

Leaning over his desk, Tom had delivered the line straight-faced. Watching Jack's face turn bright red, Wanda had to fight the giggles.

"So, about the case," Steve said, stepping in to rescue his partner, "we just came from Tall Tree Farms. We were hoping to talk to our main suspect, but he'd left to go on a trail ride."

"Don't you mean your only suspect?" Tom asked tersely as he straightened up.

"Josh Brady's our man," Jack insisted. "He was the last person to be seen with—"

Abruptly Tom held up his hand, a silent command for Jack to stop talking.

"I know the story! How can I help?"

"Uh, we just wanted to check in," Steve said quickly. "See if we've missed anything. We swung by the hospital but apparently Claudia Harris isn't there. Wondered if perhaps you could tell us where she is. We'd like to talk to her."

"She's recovering in a private facility and under my protection. The doctors have made it clear she's not ready to answer questions. I'll let you know when she is. In the meantime you probably want to check out the tavern, but after you're done there you should head back to Marionville. I'll keep you posted."

"We still have to interview Josh Brady," Jack interjected. "This is our case. He's our number one suspect."

"Ah, I see," Tom murmured. "Here I thought we were all working together. My mistake."

"We are," Steve said hastily, "and I'm sure you're busy so we'll take off, but before we go—I get the feeling you're not crazy about Brady as a suspect."

"Let me put it like this. I'd be more interested in him if the scarf hadn't shown up. Anything else?"

"No. Thanks for your time," Steve said as he and Jack rose to their feet. "We'll head out to The Horseshoe."

"Where are you boys staying?" Tom asked, standing up and shaking their hands.

"The Blue Motel."

"Ah. You might want to pick up some insect repellant."

"Mosquitos?"

"Bed bugs."

At Tom's last comment, and the expressions on the faces of the two detectives, Wanda had to drop her eyes to keep from breaking into hysterics. As they left and the door closed behind them, she could no longer contain herself.

"Seventeen and two Rottweilers? Bed bugs?" she exclaimed, laughing out loud. "You are so bad!"

"I have no idea what you're talking about," Tom said, poker-faced but with a wink. "Go light a fire under whoever's getting that title report. I want the information yesterday."

"Yes, sir," she said, still giggling as she placed the pad and pen on his desk.

"Wanda, one more thing. Get in touch with Josh Brady and make sure he stays out of sight. I need a little more time, and Steve and Jack have to be kept busy. Trying to find him will take care of that."

OVER LUNCH AT DREAM Horse Ranch, Heath discovered Theresa's new boyfriend did not match the ugly gossip. There had been no sign of the ego he'd heard about. Heath trusted his instincts, and they said Josh was a decent, trustworthy guy. But Josh had cleverly avoided any conversation about The Horseshoe Tavern and the events of the fateful night he'd hustled Theresa out of there. As lunch drew to a close and Theresa began clearing the table, Heath invited Josh to join him in the den for a few minutes.

"I'd like to show you a video of a horse I'm thinkin' about buyin'. He's back East. I don't make a habit of buyin' horses off a video, and I'm not about to start now. I'd negotiate a trial, or maybe fly out and see him, but I'd like your take."

"Sure. Be happy to give you my opinion."

"We'll be back in a minute," Heath said as they pushed back their chairs.

"Okay. I'll be here," Carly replied, knowing there was no horse video and Heath just wanted a private chat.

"Sure is a nice place you've got here," Josh remarked as they walked down the wide hallway to the den. "The layout is terrific, and that barn. Damn, it's the Taj Mahal for horses. It's so open and airy."

"Thanks, Josh. Gettin' this place to this point didn't happen overnight."

"Heath, I'm a straight-shooter, and I get the feelin' I'm walkin' in your den 'cos you wanna chat. If this is about Theresa you don't have to worry. I'll do right by her."

"I know that, and I'm not her keeper. I care about her, but what she does with her personal life is up to her."

"So, what's on your mind?"

"I was sittin' at that lunch thinkin' you're nothin' like the guy I've heard about."

"Let me guess. I'm a buzzin' bee flyin' from flower to flower, and I leave a path of broken petals."

"Along those lines, yeah, but Theresa's a sharp gal, and when she told me how you're helpin' the police I tried to recall who'd told me the bullshit. I don't mean to overstep, but I'm real curious. Did you and Duke Palmer have some kinda fallin' out?"

"Duke Palmer? I don't even know the man," Josh replied, taken aback by the question. "Why do you ask?"

"He's the guy who told me you were trouble, especially when it came to women."

"Why the hell would Duke Palmer tell you, or anyone, anything about me?"

"That's why I asked. I wondered if the two of you had a run in."

"Nope. You should ask him how he got me so wrong. Isn't he a friend of yours?"

"Not exactly. I've been to the tavern a few times and he brings his horse here when he goes off on one of his beer hunts, but we don't socialize. Before she met you I thought he and Theresa might hit it off. In fact, when he dropped his horse off a few days ago he made it a point to ask about her."

Josh ran his fingers through his hair. Heath's comment prickled the hair on the back of his neck.

"Is there something you wanna tell me about him, Josh?"

"I wish I could, but—"

"Why do I get the feelin' you think he's the one who spiked Theresa's drink?"

"Because I do," Josh said gravely. "I kept my eye on her that night. No other guys approached her, not even me. She gave off this vibe, like she was there by herself and wanted to stay that way. She sat at the bar the whole time, and he stood behind it."

"Wait a second. If you think he spiked Theresa's drink, that means he could've spiked the drink of the girl who went missin'. Damn, Josh, you think he's the dirtbag who—?"

"Dammit, that's my phone," Josh declared, interrupting him as he pulled it from his pocket. "Excuse me. I need to take this."

"Do you need privacy?"

"No, I'll make it quick. Hey, Wanda."

"Josh, don't go home."

"Don't go home?" he repeated. "Why not?"

"The detectives on the case were here. They went by Tall Tree Farms to find you, and I'm pretty sure they'll stake out your house tonight waiting for you to show up."

"Why don't I just talk to them? I have nothin' to hide."

"Not a good idea, and the captain would prefer it if you kept a low profile."

"Dang it. I guess I can check into a motel for a few days, but I'll need to go home to get some clothes."

"Do that now. They're over at the tavern and they'll probably be there a while. I shouldn't say this, but they're not the brightest bulbs in the chandelier. One especially. I don't think he even lights up."

"Is that a good thing or a bad thing?"

"Could be either, but I'm optimistic this will be over soon."

"That's good to hear. Okay, I'll zip home, then let you know where I've landed. Bye, and thanks."

"Bye."

"Hey, Josh," Heath said as Josh pushed his phone back in his pocket, "if you need a place to stay you're welcome to hang out here."

"That's real nice, but I wouldn't—"

"You know what? With Carly laid up we could use your help. We have someone startin' tomorrow, but she can only give us a couple of hours a day. Besides, you saved Theresa's neck. Let me return the favor. Do you really wanna stay in some crappy motel?"

"Not especially."

"Great. That's settled, but can I ask why you need to keep your head down? I don't care, I'm just curious, is all."

"Sure. Someone's tryin' to stitch me up, and there are a couple of ambitious detectives who have decided it would be real nice to close the Claudia Harris abduction case. Need I say more?"

"Hell no. Get to your house while the gettin's good. The gate code is one-one-one-two."

"That's easy."

"Maybe too easy," Heath said with a chuckle as they left the room and strode quickly down the hall. "I'll let Theresa know. I'll bet she'll be tickled you're stayin. Just so you know, we have plenty of room here in the house if it comes to that."

"I'll talk to Theresa. I'll let her make that decision, and thanks for the option. Man, this is one for the books. When I left medical school to throw my hat in the trainin' ring, I never thought I'd end up in a situation like this," Josh said, shaking his head as they walked out the front door. "Hey, Heath, Theresa said Duke has his horse here. Do you know when he's pickin' him up?"

"I haven't heard from him, but don't worry, when he—now it's my turn," Heath declared as his phone rang. "Speak of the devil."

"Duke?"

"Yep. You might get your answer. Hey, Duke."

"Hey, Heath. I'm headin' back early. Some asshole broke into the tavern. Can I swing by in a couple of hours?"

"Sure. I'll see you when you get here," he replied, ending the call. "That's it, Josh. Duke Palmer will be here around three o'clock."

CHAPTER TWENTY-TWO

HEATH WAS WORKING IN his office when the landline rang. Glancing at his watch and seeing the time he guessed Duke Palmer had pulled up to the gate.

"Heath Boyd speakin'."

"Hey, Heath. It's Duke. I'm at the gate."

"Come on in. I'm in the middle of somethin'. Do you need me?"

"Nope. I'll just load up my boy and be on my way. I'll pop a check in the mail like always."

"Sounds good. I'll buzz you in."

Pushing the number nine to open the gates, he replaced the receiver, then grabbed his cell phone off his desk and texted Josh.

Not sure where you are, but Palmer is rollin' in. Stay outta sight. He probably won't take long.

In the tack room fervently kissing Theresa, Josh broke away to check the incoming message.

"Anything important?" Theresa asked, her arms still wrapped around his waist.

"Duke Palmer just arrived to pick up his horse."

"Talk about bad timing."

"Hold on," he said, freeing her so he could use both hands. "I need to text him back."

Thanks. I'm in the barn with Theresa. I'll stay put.

"I thought he wasn't coming until three."

"That was a guesstimate," Josh replied, moving away to look through the window. "There he is, and he's stoppin' real close to where I parked my two-horse."

"I wish Andy and Salvo were here."

"Hopefully he'll just load up and leave. Dammit. I've lost sight of him. He must've walked around the back to open the doors."

"I don't like him wandering around like that," Theresa remarked. "What if he recognizes your truck? If he is behind this crazy plan to set you up, he'll call the police the minute he leaves. Maybe even before."

"I think you're bein' paranoid."

"Being paranoid isn't necessarily a bad thing," she said, heading towards the door. "I'll keep watch by the entrance to the barn. I can let you know if he's coming this way."

"Theresa, make sure you stay away from him."

"I have no desire to speak to the man. I'll just keep an eye on him."

"I don't want him to see you."

"He won't! Lock the door behind me!"

"Damn, you're stubborn," he muttered as she disappeared into the barn aisle, then abruptly decided she was right. If Duke had planted the scarf in the trailer, he could well recognize the truck that had been hooked up to it. "I hate this shit," he muttered, turning the deadbolt. "I hope Wanda's right. I hope this is over soon."

Theresa had reached the end of the barn, and peering around the corner the cold hand of fear clutched her chest. Duke had passed the trailers and was marching towards Josh's white truck in the parking area.

A flash of movement caught the corner of her eye.

Darting her head, she sucked in the air, then broke into a sprint towards Queenie's paddock.

The big mare was galloping towards the fence.

Theresa knew exactly what she was about to do.

"Don't, Queenie," she wailed, waving her arms. "Stop. Stop."

But the horse didn't hear her, or chose to ignore the frantic plea, and lifting off the ground she cleared the fence by a mile.

Theresa quickly realized there was only one thing she could do.

Spinning around, she raced towards the parking area.

The clattering of hooves echoed through the air as Queenie made a beeline for her prey. In the tack room Josh could hear the sounds, but from his vantage point he couldn't see anything. Then abruptly his mare appeared galloping around Heath's horse van, leaning into the turn like a motorbike on a speedway. Quickly scanning the parking lot, Josh finally saw Duke frantically looking around for the loose horse. Josh shot his eyes back to Queenie. She'd broken to a trot, and with nostrils flaring and head down, she was advancing towards her target. Suddenly seeing her, Duke's wide-eyed look of panic signaled his realization that Queenie was after him. In a panic he stumbled backwards, then letting out a cry he took off.

"No. Whoa. Whoa!" Theresa yelled, sprinting into view and placing herself between the mare and the man running for his life.

Snorting and tossing her head, Queenie slowed down, then stopped and pawed the ground.

"Hey, sweet girl. Not a good plan," Theresa exclaimed, walking slowly towards her. "You'll get taken away from us. You can't do things like this."

"What the fuck is wrong with that fuckin' horse?" Duke yelled, popping up from behind Andy's SUV parked nearby. "You should shoot the damn thing."

"Something scared her," Theresa called back. "She was spooked."

"Bullshit. She was comin' after me."

"She hasn't been here very long and I think there was a bobcat in the tree at the edge of her paddock."

"A bobcat?"

"One ran out when I put her there this morning. Come on, sweet girl," Theresa said calmly. "I'll take you back. Would you rather go to your stall and have some hay?"

Able to hear and see everything, Josh watched in relieved disbelief. Theresa had begun moving towards the paddocks, and though tossing her head, Queenie dutifully followed.

STANDING AT THE WINDOW of his office, Heath had been mesmerized. But torn. Though his first impulse had been to dash from his office to help, he'd wanted to witness the events. If anyone was injured, or vehicles damaged, he'd be able to give an honest, eye-witness account, then it had hit him. His word may not be enough. Grabbing his phone, he'd recorded the entire episode.

"Carly's not gonna believe this," he muttered, and walking hastily from his office, he hurried into their bedroom. On the bed with ice on her bruised side, she looked up at him expectantly.

"Did I just hear something?"

"You sure did. Check this out," he said, handing her the phone. "I've gotta go down to the barn. Stay put."

"This is so annoying."

"I know, but you won't get better any faster by ignorin' the doctor's orders, or mine."

Kissing her quickly, he strode from the room, and quickly made his way down the hall and out the front door. Jumping in his ATV he headed down the driveway, immediately spying Duke loading his gelding, but there was no sign of Theresa or Queenie. Assuming they were safely inside the barn, he drove straight across to talk with Duke.

"Hey, I heard some noise from the house. Is everything okay down here?"

"That's some wild mare Theresa has," Duke said, feigning a limp as he closed up the back of the trailer. "The horse jumped out of her paddock and came after me."

"Really?"

"I'm sorry, Heath, but we're gonna have to talk about this. I fell over and twisted my back, and my knee is all messed up."

"Where did this happen?"

"Over there by that white truck."

"Uh-huh."

"I'll need to talk to Theresa as well. That mare should be put down. She couldn't control it."

"I couldn't help but notice you have no shavin's in that trailer. Would you like me to grab you a bag?"

"We don't have far to go. It's no big deal. Thanks though. I'll call you about all this. Right now I just wanna get home and shower, then I'll go see a doctor."

"Good idea. If he wants to see how you fell have him get in touch with me. I have security cameras all over this place so the incident would have been recorded from several different angles. I'll check out the footage right now. What's the matter, Duke? You look like you just realized your zipper's down and that's why the girls are gigglin."

"I, uh, I just remembered something. I need to go. Thanks. I'll be in touch."

"Take care now. A bath in Epsom salts wouldn't hurt. I'm gonna check on Theresa and her horse."

"Yeah, okay. Bye, Heath."

Driving away, Heath glanced over his shoulder. Walking normally, Duke had reached his truck and was climbing inside. Now fully aware of Duke's true nature, Heath stopped his ATV. Only when Duke Palmer had left the property and the gates had closed behind him did Heath continue into the barn.

THE MOMENT JOSH HAD seen Heath head down to speak with Duke, he'd hurriedly unbolted the tack room door, and stepped into the barn aisle. He'd found Theresa and Queenie locked in a hug.

"Talk about double trouble," he murmured walking toward them. "You both gave me a heart attack. Shame on you, Queenie, and as for you, young lady!"

"As for me, what?" she retorted, releasing the mare's neck and staring up at him with challenge in her eyes. "I had to stop her. I couldn't just let her mow that asshole down. He would've sued Heath, and you, and God only knows what would've happened to Queenie."

"But—"

"But nothing. You can scold me all you want, I'd do the same thing again."

"What about you, Queenie? You're the one who started all this. Jumping over that fence and goin' after that man."

Lifting her head high in the air, she pulled back her upper lip as though smelling something foul. As upset and worried as he was, Josh couldn't help but laugh.

"Yeah, okay, very funny. He's a piece of stinky cow dung, but please don't do that again."

"She was protecting you," Theresa exclaimed. "Duke was about to check out your truck."

"So let him. I've got nothin' to hide. So what if those dickhead detectives find me here. I'm not into sneakin' around. I'm done."

"No, don't say that."

"Why not?"

"Because then...uh..."

"Ah, gotcha. Then I'd be leavin' here."

"Please don't go. At least stay the night. Maybe there are reasons Wanda doesn't want you to surface that you don't know about."

"You might have a point, and I definitely wanna spend the night with you."

"Thank you," she beamed, stepping up to him and throwing her arms around his neck. "I love—uh—that you're going to be here."

"Me too, Princess," he murmured, loving the feel of her body against his. "What about you, Queenie. Do you wanna go back in your paddock? That bad man has probably left by now."

"Yep, he's gone," Heath declared, walking into the barn. "That was quite a show. You'll be happy to know I video'd the whole thing, and it's just as well I did, but, uh, this naughty mare doesn't have a halter on. After that display don't you think that might be a good idea?"

"He's right, Theresa," Josh said firmly. "I should've told you the minute I saw you. Put a halter on."

"I'll just take her back to the paddock."

"With a halter and lead rope," Heath repeated, lifting one off a stall door. "Here."

"Okay," she said with a sigh, slipping it over the mare's head. "I'll be right back. Come on, sweet girl. I think you're a total superstar. Just ignore them."

"Man, oh, man, Josh, you sure are gonna have your hands full with that pair."

"I already do, and I'm real sorry about what happened."

"Josh, I gotta say, I've been around horses since I was a kid, and I've never seen anything like that. Your mare was gonna kill Duke Palmer. And Theresa, no experience, supposedly terrified of horses until she met your mare, walked right up and stopped the chaos. I'm both dumbfounded and confounded. Has Queenie ever shown signs of aggression like that before? She jumped over that fence to go after him! I'm still shakin' my head."

"I almost got into a fight once, and yeah, she did, but Queenie's not like a horse. I mean, she is, but there's more to her. Way more. She took to Theresa right off, and as you know, their connection was mutual. I honestly don't know what to make of her, but I've stopped tryin' to figure her out. I just consider myself blessed that she picked me."

"She picked you?"

"Oh, yeah. For sure. I'll tell you the story one day."

"How old is she? Do you know anything about her background?"

"Both good questions, but you won't like the answer to the first one. I have no clue about her age. As to her history, nothin' there either."

"But her teeth. Surely you can read her age from her teeth."

"Go ahead and try. Have your vet try."

"No sign of a Galvayne's groove?"

"Not yet, and they haven't changed since the day I got her. It's as if she has a magic elixir of youth stashed away somewhere. Anyway, I'm real sorry, and unless that creep comes back, I don't think you'll see anything like that again. Speakin' of Duke, what were you sayin' about the video?"

"Yeah, the video. I don't know if that jackass is the one who spiked Theresa's drink or not, but he's a slimy sonofabitch. He tried to tell me he'd taken a fall when Queenie chased him and his back and knee were hurtin. Said he was off to see his doctor."

"No shit. What a scumbag."

"Yep. I told him this place had security cameras if his doctor needed to see them. That shut him up. He hightailed it outta here real quick."

"I'll bet he did."

"I'm goin' back to the house. I've still got a pile of work with my name on it, but I'll see you later. Oh, by the way, I saw you ridin' Chuck. Real glad to see that."

"He was fine. That bitless bridle will be good for him. He'll be a bit sensitive about his mouth for a while, not 'cos of any pain, just memory."

"Yeah, I figured. I'm gonna have to have a talk with Carly about all that when she's better. I told her to wait," he muttered, staring at the ground, then raising his eyes, he added, "I know you're a full-time trainer with your own business, but do you have time to give me a few hours a week until Carly's back up? Sandy's fine, but she's just an exercise rider. Carly and Andy are my trainers."

"No problem. My busy times are late afternoons and weekends. I school the horses in the mornin, so there's a lull in the early afternoon, speakin' of which, I'm gonna go back to Tall Tree tomorrow. I've got a business to run."

"That's up to you, but I'd talk to your police friends before you do. Get all the facts."

"Theresa said the same thing."

"Yeah, this is a time to play it smart, not be impatient."

CLOSING THE FILE FOLDER, Tom Lewis smiled triumphantly, then picking up his luxury items one- by-one, he savored their smells. He'd smoke the cigar as he drank the whiskey, then devour the rich chocolate treats over the course of the evening.

"This win could be one of the most satisfying of my career," he murmured, reaching for his desk phone. "Wanda? Come in to my office."

"Now, sir?"

"No, five minutes ago."

"I'll be right there."

Pulling out his stop watch he clicked the top, watched the second hand move, then clicked it again when the knock came on the door and Wanda poked her head in.

"Hit the chair."

"How hard?"

"You're spending too much time around me," he said with a chuckle. "Are you doing anything tonight?"

"No, sir."

"You are now. There's a thermos in my souvenir cabinet. Fill it with coffee, decent coffee from Maureen's cafe, not the shit we have here," he ordered, pulling out his wallet and handing her a fifty-dollar bill. "Buy whatever obscene cakes you want, and don't scrimp. They may have to last us a while."

"Yes, sir," she said excitedly. "May I ask?"

"Yep, when we're on our way. And your response time has improved by three-seconds. Keep it up and pretty soon you'll be walking through that door before I hang up the phone."

She stared at him for a moment, then rolling her eyes, she headed out. He was irascible, impossible, demanding and difficult to please, but she wouldn't change a thing about him.

CHAPTER TWENTY-THREE

DURING DINNER ANDY and Salvo had continuously watched the video of the remarkable scene, and Salvo had emailed the footage to himself, exclaiming he wanted to upload it on to YouTube.

"This would go viral. We'd make a bunch of money."

"And get our asses sued," Heath remarked. "Sorry, Salvo, but I don't want Dream Horse Ranch to become famous for out of control horses trying to kill guests."

"No-one will know this happened here, and we don't need Duke Palmer's permission to put it up. I know about this stuff, and you can't really see his face—well—except for that moment when Queenie drops her head and starts snorting. He looks like he peed his pants."

"Maybe he did."

Carly had made the quip, then started giggling. A series of rude comments followed until Theresa began clearing the table. Though she had enjoyed making fun of the vile Duke Palmer, weariness had set in. She needed a shower, and to crawl into bed for a long snuggle with her cowboy. Salvo and Josh helped her clean up, and they were soon heading to their cabins in the Land Rover.

With the small shower stall in the cabin unable to accommodate two people, Theresa showered first, and climbing between the sheets, she let out a heavy sigh and sank into the mattress. The long, dramatic day had finally come to an end, and surrendering to a long yawn, she closed her eyes.

"Josh?" she mumbled, suddenly aware of his body against hers. "I must have fallen asleep. I'm so glad you're here."

"Me too. I have a surprise for you, but you're probably too tired."

"I don't think a girl is ever too tired for a surprise," she purred, moving her hand across his chest and down his muscled arms. "I love your body."

"The feelin's mutual."

"What's the surprise?"

"You're exhausted. It can wait."

"No, I don't want to wait."

"You're sure?"

"I am absolutely, one-thousand percent, positively sure."

"You have to close your eyes and keep them closed, no matter what."

"Ooh, I like this already."

"I didn't hear a promise."

"I promise to close my eyes and keep them closed, no matter what," she said, squeezing them shut.

"I'm gonna roll back the bedcovers, and you're gonna bend your knees up, then lock your hands together behind your head."

"This is a lot of work for a surprise."

"Bendin' your knees and puttin' your hands behind your head is a lotta work?"

"It is at the moment."

"You wanna stop?"

"No!"

Slipping from the bed, Josh moved across the room and opened his overnight bag. When he'd packed his clothes he'd also picked up a few of his favorite toys. Retrieving an oddly-shaped, very thin, vibrating tube with a remote control, and a seagull's feather, he returned to the bed.

"Lift your hips, Princess." Grabbing a pillow, he stuffed it under her hips as she raised herself up. "Stay just like that," he said softly, sliding his fingers into her pussy. "Already so wet? How did that happen?"

"Being naked with you makes me so hot. Ooh, that feels wonderful."

Slowly pushing his finger into her womanhood, he searched out her ultra-sensitive area and softly massaged. Listening to her grateful moans, he began testing for pressure sensitivity, then withdrew and picked up the tube.

"Why did you stop?"

"Your surprise is coming."

Placing the tube at her entrance, he observed her face as he cautiously moved it forward. At the first gasp, he paused, then continued until the slim device was fully inserted.

"How does that feel?"

"Strange, but good, really good."

"All you need to do is feel. Are you ready?"

"I have no idea. What are you going to do?"

"Nothing if you don't relax and accept."

"Sorry."

"Take a deep breath and let it out. There you go. This is going to feel different, but very quickly there will be incredible pleasure."

Picking up the remote control, he moved the setting to low and pressed the power button, then taking the seagull's feather, he danced it against her clit.

"Josh, Josh, ooh, Josh. What's happening? Oh, that's, that's..."

"Ssh, ride it, Princess," he softly crooned. "You won't come yet, you'll just ride the wave."

"That tickling, it's so bad and so good. I feel...," she mumbled, but as the sensations swept her away, her voice trailed off.

Wrapping the fingers of his free hand around his rigid cock, he stroked himself as he watched. Color was filling her chest and neck, her breathing was quick, and her soft cries sounded more like a song than moans of pleasure.

"I need to come," she suddenly bleated. "Why can't I come? I need to. I need to."

The feather against her clit, and the thin tube vibrating against the magic spot on her inner wall were just enough to keep her on the edge.

"I know, babe," he purred. "Be patient."

"I can't, I really can't."

With a knowing smile, he stopped the attention to her clit and increased the intensity of the vibrator to medium, but as she arched her back and held her breath, he turned the dial back down to low.

"Please, I'm begging you," she gasped, "I'll die if you don't let me come."

"We can't have that," he crooned, softly rubbing his finger against her clit. "Very soon. Just give me a moment and enjoy the sweet torture."

She moaned loudly, but slipping from the bed, he returned the feather to his bag and pulled out a fresh package of condoms. He'd stopped at the pharmacy on his way back to the ranch, thinking the quick trip into the store only a small risk that offered a much needed reward. Ripping off the condom wrapper, he slid the thin membrane over his cock and returned to the bed.

"How much do you want me?"

"So much," she whimpered. "More than I can say."

"I'm going to slide inside you, but you have to be very still, then you're going to come very, very hard."

"I know, I can feel it."

"Princess, you have no idea."

Placing himself against her entrance, being careful not to dislodge the placement of the narrow vibrating tube, he slowly pushed forward. As the divine sensation pulsed against his cock, he picked up the control and moved the dial to medium. Her immediate cry joined with his deep groan, and though he couldn't thrust, he didn't need to. As he lowered his mouth to draw in a nipple, the unique device rocketed them into their orgasms, not mighty eruptions, but ongoing scintillating waves of intense pleasure. Even after Josh had released and his flaccid member rested inside her, the delicious spasms continued to ripple through his body.

But he had to bring her multiple orgasms to an end, and reluctantly lifting his mouth from her breast, he reached for the remote. As he lowered the speed, her cries lessened and her taut muscles eased, then switching it off, her body finally fell limp. Slipping from her depths, he carefully withdrew the tube and moved the pillow from under her hips.

Floating on a soft, pink, fluffy cloud, Theresa had never known such intense pleasure or sublime bliss. When she felt the covers move across her, she realized her hands were still behind her head.

"What was that?" she mumbled, unlocking her fingers and moving her arms down.

"Just a little something I invented."

"You invented?"

"Yep. Go to sleep, Princess."

"Will you show it to me?"

"In the mornin'."

"Why? I mean, why did you invent it?"

"Horse trainin' doesn't pay real well unless you hit the big time. Now go to sleep."

"You are amazing," she whimpered, and though more questions buzzed through her brain, those became her last words as she surrendered to the sandman.

BEHIND THE WHEEL OF an unmarked black Ford Explorer parked on the shoulder of the road just past Tall Tree Farms, Captain Tom Lewis was enjoying a blueberry muffin.

"You're thinking this is a waste of time," he remarked. "I can hear the grumbling between your ears."

"We've been here five hours," Wanda replied.

"Six."

"Six?"

"Six. I let you nap for an hour. You thought it was five minutes."

"Shit."

"Rats come out at night. You have to be patient. I sat on the second floor of a warehouse waiting for a suspect for three days."

"Did he ever show up?"

"He was already there," Tom said with a chuckle. "When we switched shifts with the team who'd been there before us, we missed him."

"You're kidding?"

"Nope, but we got him coming out."

"I feel like I've been sitting in this car for a week," she muttered. "You're sure about this."

"I hope that was a statement and not a question," he said briskly, then suddenly glanced in the rearview mirror. "Well, well, I do believe the vermin has surfaced."

"Is the car driving into Tall Tree?" she asked, turning her head to look out the back window. "It is! Thank God. Now what?"

"Now you stay put."

"What? Where are you going?"

"To take a walk on the wild side. Don't go anywhere."

Heart pounding, Wanda watched him jog across the road, but with no streetlights, and only a crescent moon, he quickly disappeared from view.

"He knows what he's doing," she muttered to herself, then quietly added, "I hope."

Fifteen minutes felt like an hour, and when his tall form reappeared striding confidently across the field, she almost cried with relief.

"Is everything okay?" she asked as he slid back behind the wheel.

"Any reason it wouldn't be?"

"What were you doing?"

"Here," he replied, handing her his phone.

"I'm looking at a map."

"Correct. And soon a red dot will appear and start to move."

AN HOUR LATER, ACROSS the street from Josh's house, Detective Steve Yates was reading a book while Jack Collins watched porn on his iPad. They'd been there for almost seven hours, and yawning heavily, Steve closed his novel and leaned back his head.

"I don't think he's coming home."

"Yeah, you might be right," Jack agreed.

"Let's call it a night. I need to sleep, bed bugs or no bed bugs."

"Fifteen more minutes."

"Why?"

"That's how long this movie has left. I want to see how it ends."

"Uh, you know how it ends," Steve retorted. "The guys will shoot their wad and the girls will scream in ecstasy."

"Not this one. I think Rhonda's going to spank Julie for borrowing her pink bra. I've got to see that."

Closing his eyes, Steve silently counted to ten, asked God why he had Jack as a partner, then decided to nod off.

Neither of them noticed a man step from a car that had stopped halfway down the block. Nor did they see him amble towards Josh's house, jump the fence and move around to the back.

SITTING ASTRIDE QUEENIE, Theresa was galloping across a lush green meadow, but the verdant grass gave way to a thicket. The mare slowed to a trot, then a walk as she entered the trees. Birds were singing, and the sun shone through the canopy of branches, but when they came out the other side, she saw a horse trailer. The doors were wide open. There were no shavings on the floor, and no hay in the feed compartment. Shards of wood and broken glass littered the ground, and in the distance she could see The Horseshoe Tavern, though one side of the building appeared to be distorted.

"Queenie, why did you bring me here?"

"You must tell Josh what you see."

"Theresa. Wake up. Theresa."

His voice seemed far away, then suddenly her eyes popped open.

"Josh?"

"You're safe," he said softly, holding her tightly. "It was just a dream."

"I have to tell you..."

"You can tell me in the mornin.'"

"It can't wait," she said urgently, shifting in his arms to look up at him. "Queenie said I have to tell you and I don't want to forget."

"Okay, Princess. If it will help you go back to sleep."

"We were in a field surrounded by trees. There was a trailer, but it had no shavings on the floor or hay in the feeder. I don't know why, but that's important. On the ground were these wooden boards. Not big, but thin strips. Broken glass too, and across the field I could see The Horseshoe Tavern, but the side of it was sort of bulging. Do you have any idea what that means?"

"Of course," he exclaimed, slapping his forehead. "That's what I couldn't put my finger on. That's it. Theresa, you're a genius."

"I didn't do anything. I just had a dream. Queenie. It was Queenie who took me there."

"I don't understand, but I don't need to. This is it! I have the answer."

CHAPTER TWENTY-FOUR

A SOFT KISS ON HER cheek, and the word *Princess* whispered in her ear, woke Theresa from a deep sleep.

"I've gotta go. Wanda and the captain are pickin' me up."

"They are? Why? What time is it?" she asked, half-opening her eyes.

"Six-thirty. I didn't wanna leave without sayin' goodbye, and tellin' you it was Duke Palmer who spiked your drink."

"Huh. Why am I not surprised? Wait, where are you going?"

"To The Horseshoe Tavern."

"I'll come with you."

"No, you stay here. I'll explain everything later, and I've already spoken to Heath. Bye, Princess. I'll call you when I can," he promised, then kissing her softly, he added, "love you."

It wasn't until he'd left, and she'd settled down for a few more minutes of sleep, that the words sunk in.

Her eyes flew open. Abruptly sitting up she stared at the door.

"Did I dream that? No. He definitely said it. But did he mean, love you, like, I love you, or was it more like, take care or have a nice day? Shit."

Though she had no answer, a happy smile curled the edges of her lips. Knowing she'd never be able to go back to sleep, she left the bed and headed into the shower.

Walking briskly down the driveway, adrenalin pumping through his veins with the pending drama of the morning ahead, it was the two words Josh had uttered sitting in the forefront of his mind. They'd spilled off his lips with no thought, but as he neared the gate, the black Dodge Charger waiting on the other side, an epiphany swept over him.

He did love her.

Was in love with her.

He loved her smile, the ever-present challenge in her dark enigmatic eyes, her courage, but mostly he loved her huge heart.

A honk snapped him from his thoughts. Realizing he was standing stock still, he broke into a jog, pressed the buzzer to open the pedestrian gate, and hurrying across to the car, he climbed in the back seat.

"Did you run into an invisible wall?" Wanda asked as Tom hit the accelerator. "Why did you stop?"

"A sudden thought."

"Okay, son, let's have it. I don't take kindly to having my feet held to the fire. I could arrest you for perverting the cause of justice, withholding evidence, obstruction, and I could probably add a few more charges into the mix."

"But you won't."

"How can you be so sure?"

"First off, you wanna catch this guy probably more than anyone, and goin' through all that shit will cost valuable time. Second, you know how many hours I've given to this case and in your heart you know I deserve to be there. Third, even though you maintain a tough, gruff exterior, you're not a jerk, and only a jerk would do somethin' like that."

"You got me," Tom said with a wry grin, staring at Josh in the rearview mirror. "Now tell me what you know."

"You promise you won't pull to the side of the road and kick me to the curb?"

"Only a jerk would do that."

"Touché."

"Don't worry, you're coming along for the ride. Now tell me why I had to wake up a judge and convince him to give me a search warrant, and why three of my best boys are waiting at the tavern."

"Wanda, remember that cable that led nowhere, and those crates of wine and beer pressed up against the wall?"

"Of course."

"Behind them is a hidden space. At least, I'm pretty sure there is."

"You don't know?" Tom said gravely. "This is a guess?"

"More than a guess. The room behind the bar is really narrow, and when I stepped outside and looked back at the buildin', I had an itch I couldn't scratch, but for the life of me I couldn't figure out what was botherin' me. I woke up last night with the answer. That room doesn't extend to the end of the buildin', so what's there? Then something else hit me. Why would you go away and leave hundreds of dollars of stock so vulnerable? Those crates were just sittin' there, along with all the booze on the shelves. Everyone knew he'd left town."

"Bottom line, he's got a hidden space and you don't think he went anywhere."

"That's exactly what I think. And his trailer. There's something up with that as well. When I brought my mare over to the ranch yesterday, Carly suggested I unhook my trailer and leave it there. Made sense. Freed up my vehicle, but when Duke showed up to collect his horse, he rolled in with his trailer. Now I've gotta ask myself, why didn't he leave it there. Why would he haul his trailer on a trip that's about findin' new beer?"

"Maybe he has another vehicle," Wanda suggested.

"Maybe, but that still doesn't explain why he wouldn't leave his trailer where his horse is."

"You've got a mechanical brain, son. That's smart thinking. Wanda, call the station. Have that truck and trailer impounded."

"Yes, sir."

"What's a mechanical brain?" Josh asked. "If I've got one, I'd like to know what it is."

"You have a way of breaking down information and seeing how the parts fit in the bigger picture. Anything else you've figured out?"

"That's it for the moment."

"How do you think that scarf ended up in your trailer?"

"That's stumped me," Josh muttered. "Not how it was done, that's easy. It's the why that I find so puzzlin'. Why would someone as smart as Duke Palmer do something so stupid?"

"That's the right question," Tom said as he turned off the main road and started down the street to the lake turnoff. "Tell me the answer."

"Have you come up with it?"

"Yep. Think about it. Repeat the question just the way you put it. See what you deduce by the time we get to the tavern. We're about three minutes away."

"He loves to do this," Wanda said with a grin. "He does it to me all the time."

"And look how much smarter you are because of it," Tom said, shooting her a wink.

"I just had a thought," Josh said, alarm in his voice. "Do we know where Duke Palmer is? Aren't you worried about him taking off? If you impound his—"

"You don't have to worry. Wanda and I took care of that last night."

"I don't understand."

"I'll explain later. The tavern's a minute away," he continued, moving on to the gravel road. "Have you got that answer yet?"

"It's impossible. Why would someone as smart as Duke Palmer do something so stupid? He wouldn't."

"There you go!" the captain exclaimed as he drove into the parking lot and came to a stop. "He wouldn't. So who would?"

"Are you suggestin' he has a partner?"

"I'm not suggesting anything. He has a partner. A stupid partner. Not unheard of in these serial offenders."

"Who is it? Do you know?"

"Of course," Tom replied getting out of the car, "but I'll let you ponder that for a bit."

"See," Wanda said with a grin. "I told you. He does it all the time, but only because he likes you. I think you can consider yourself officially adopted."

"Sam?" Josh muttered. "He could've easily put that scarf in my trailer, and he does some really dumb things at times. Damn."

"Earth to Josh. Are you coming?"

"What? Sorry," he apologized, finding Wanda holding his door open. "The only person comin' to mind is the barn manager at Tall Tree. He's always struck me as a bit odd and not very bright, but thinkin' about him bein' a part of this really bothers me."

"That's because he's someone you work with, someone you're around every day, someone who fed your horse," she said, handing him a pair of latex gloves.

"Oh, no!"

"What? Did a penny drop?"

"Kinda, but I wanna focus on that space behind the crates," he said quickly, silently thinking, *Is that why Queenie was so anxious to get outta that place?*

"Hey, Josh, you were right," the captain called. "Get over here."

He quickened his step, but as he hurried forward, Wanda's phone rang.

"I need to get this," she declared, staring at the screen. "Go ahead."

Breaking into a jog, he arrived just in time to see two burly young police officers rolling the tall pile of crates away from the wall.

"What the hell?"

"Yep. Only the top two contained bottles. All the ones underneath are a facade. What have we got here?"

"The wall looks solid, captain," one of the officers said, "but there's a cable going through just above the baseboard."

"That's the cable that Wanda and I followed," Josh remarked. "It's connected to a unit on a shelf under the bar, but why put all this in front of a wall if there's nothin' to hide? There's no door, not even a small openin'."

"If it's not the wall," Tom mumbled, "what about—"

"The floor!" Josh exclaimed, dropping his eyes to his feet. "Look."

A large square seam boasted a tiny thumbhole, and quickly dropping to his knees, Josh slipped his finger through it and pulled. It didn't budge.

"Josh, do you see any hinges?" the captain demanded. "Slide the damn thing."

"Wait. Do you hear that?"

"Sounds like a whining dog," one of the young officers mumbled.

"Holy crap. Slide it, quick," Tom shouted. "Dammit slide it, Josh!"

"I'm trying"

It abruptly moved, and as Josh stared down into the dimly lit space he saw the form of a person curled into a fetal position.

"Call an ambulance," he said urgently. "I'm going down."

"Hold on, Josh, you—"

"I can help her. I was pre-med, remember? Shit, there's no ladder. It doesn't look far. I can drop."

Before the words had left his mouth, he had swung his legs into the opening and let himself fall.

"Stand back," Tom called. "Here's a flashlight."

The heavy-duty flashlight hit the floor, and picking it up, Josh shone the beam across the body.

"No, please don't hurt me," the young woman sobbed, curling herself into an even tighter ball. "Please let me go. I won't tell anyone, I swear I won't."

"I'm not here to hurt you," Josh said softly, feeling a wave of emotion wash through his heart. "That's over. I'm with the police. I'm here to get you out."

THOUGH DUKE HAD AVOIDED taking women from his tavern, when the dark-haired girl in the leather jacket sat on his barstool, she was almost too tempting to pass up. When she'd made it clear she only had eyes for Josh Brady, Duke had seen red. The good-looking cowboy had more women than a sheik's harem, and Theresa's exclamation had pushed Duke over the edge. Theresa would be his next victim.

But Josh Brady had beaten him to the punch.

Ten minutes after Duke had slipped the drug in her drink, Brady had hustled her out of his bar. Frustrated and angry, Duke needed a woman, and sick of seeing Josh get all the attention, Duke decided to take the buxom redhead and make sure Josh Brady got the blame.

Though she had already left, it was easy to slip into the back room and out the side door, then catch her attention. Once she'd hurried over to see what he needed, there had been no problem keeping her silent with a knife at her throat. Getting her into the subterranean hold hadn't been easy, but the noise of the tavern covered her pleas as he'd shoved her through the opening.

Stitching up Josh Brady had been going well, until Sam had decided to help things along by placing the redhead's blue scarf into Josh's trailer. The moment Sam had told him, Duke knew things could unravel, but he'd been extremely careful, and there was nothing that pointed to him.

He'd make the police decide between Sam and Josh.

The first thing he needed to do was take care of his idiot partner. The dope would fold like a flag under questioning.

Visiting Sam at Tall Tree Farms the night before, he'd handed him a wad of cash and convinced him to take off until things cooled down. With his help, Sam had written a note saying a family crisis had called him away, but he'd be in touch very soon. Persuading him to leave in the dead of night and take the mountain road rather than the freeway had been easy.

Sam hadn't made it very far.

Duke had tampered with the brakes of Sam's pickup, and at the bottom of a gorge his lifeless body was surrounded by broken metal. There had been no-one on the dark empty road to witness the horrific crash.

But now Duke was suddenly faced with his biggest problem yet.

The police closure of the tavern had been a gift. He'd nabbed his latest prize, and with no worries of unexpected visitors he'd dumped her in his special hideaway. He always left his victims alone for at least eighteen hours. It weakened and scared them, then he'd put them in his horse trailer and cart them away to an isolated spot. Any accidental passersby would assume someone was out for a nighttime ride.

Returning at sunrise with his truck and trailer to collect her, he'd just parked in the hidden clearing in front of the tavern when two police cars rolled up. He couldn't leave until they did. Hidden by the trees in the spot Sam would use to watch their girls stagger out, then nab them and keep them until the tavern closed, Duke watched and waited.

Then Josh arrived with the police Captain.

Duke broke into a sweat.

When the ambulance arrived he knew he had to run.

As he began hurriedly moving through the trees, the evil Gods sent him an unexpected gift.

Stopped by police tape stretched across the gravel road, Theresa Cavalleri was stepping from her Land Rover.

CHAPTER TWENTY-FIVE

AS DUKE PALMER STUDIED his prey, his devious mind clicked into gear.

Though she wouldn't be seen by anyone at the tavern until she reached the bend in the road, she'd only have to walk a short distance to reach it. The day was quiet. No wind, no rain, nothing to break nature's silence. Screams would be heard. He had to assume she knew he wasn't the happy-go-lucky bartender she'd chatted with. He couldn't walk up with a friendly smile and charm her as he'd done so many others. He'd have to pounce from behind, smother her mouth, and throw her in the vehicle.

But his plotting came to a sudden stop.

She'd started to walk, but after a few steps she paused, looked over her shoulder, then turned around, smiled broadly and waved.

He couldn't see down the road from his vantage point, and he risked three furtive steps to get closer to the road. Seeing and hearing nothing, his eyes snapped back to her.

His prey was gone.

He held his breath, listening keenly.

A tiny sound to his left. His upper lip curled in a sneer. The stupid girl had run into the trees. He had her now. This was his territory.

THERESA HAD THREE DISTINCT advantages.

Growing up on the rough streets of the inner city, she didn't scare easily.

She knew how to survive.

A guardian angel watched over her.

When she'd climbed from the car she'd felt uneasy, and walking down the road she could feel eyes following her. She'd become a target! To walk any further would be deadly. Action. She needed to take action, but what?

Lifting her phone from her pocket and attempting to call Josh would take too much time. A scream would bring people running, but only if they heard her. If they didn't, a scream could prove disastrous. The bend in the road wasn't far, but if her stalker was Duke Palmer she probably couldn't outrun him. He wasn't tall, but he was sinewy, and she guessed he'd be quick. Only one option remained. Hide.

The trees? No. She might lose her sense of direction and he probably knew the forest. The only other choice, the Land Rover. As an idea sprang to mind, a glimmer of hope took hold, but success depended on only one thing. Timing. She had to guess right.

Taking a breath, she turned around, broke into a huge smile, waved. Waiting only a split second, she scurried to the front of the SUV, picked up a stone and hurled it into the trees.

IN THE TAVERN PARKING lot, Wanda searched frantically for her captain. She'd tried calling, but his phone had gone straight to voice mail, and he hadn't responded to her text.

"Where's the captain?" she demanded urgently, rushing into the room behind the tavern.

"Down there with the paramedics," the young officer replied, nodding towards the opening in the floor.

"Captain?" she called, leaning over and trying to catch sight of him.

"He's gone into the tunnel," one of the paramedics replied, staring up at her. "We're about ready to move the patient. If you want to go after him you need to come down now."

A ladder had been put in place, and quickly turning around, she descended into the grimy space. Bright lights had been set up showing the passageway, but still finding it forbidding she moved with caution. The journey, however, was surprisingly short. The 'tunnel' only looked like a tunnel. It was only a few yards long and led to a door. Pushing it open she found herself in a large basement with a remarkably high ceiling. Two large monitors sat against a wall, one blank, the other showing the ugly space where the victims had been held.

"Wanda? What are you doing here?" the captain asked moving up to her.

"This place..." she stammered, aghast at what she was seeing. "A bed? Refrigerator?"

"We found their trophy stash. They've been busy."

"I think I'm going to be sick."

"Get a grip, sergeant," he said briskly. "Focus. Something sent you after me. What is it?"

"Sorry, sir. When the tow truck arrived at the location I'd given them for Palmer's truck and trailer both were gone. I pulled up the GPS and I found the truck here."

"Here? At the tavern?"

"Yes, sir. He must have driven away after I gave out the address."

"Why didn't you call or text me?"

"I tried, but the call went to voice mail, and you didn't answer my text."

"Christ. We must not have a signal down here."

"Can I help?" Josh asked. Standing nearby, he'd overheard the conversation. "I need to go up anyway. I promised Theresa I'd call her. She'll be anxious by now."

"You can't help, but you don't need to be down here. Get some air and call your girl, but don't chase anyone or take it into your head that you're an officer. You're not. Understood?"

"Not to worry. I'll be a model citizen."

"Wanda, as soon as you get up top take Dan and Mike over to that clearing. There's nowhere else he could put a truck and trailer and not be seen, but be careful."

"Yes, sir. Is there no other way in or out of here?"

"Not that I've found. Now get back up there and find that truck."

A FEW SECONDS AFTER throwing the stone, Theresa heard a faint noise, and though it could have been anything, she decided it was her stalker moving into the woods to find her. Pulse racing, she opened her bag and grabbed her phone. She was about to call Josh, but afraid her voice might carry through the quiet, she sent him an urgent text.

HELP. STOPPED BY POLICE TAPE ON ROAD. HIDING BEHIND LAND ROVER. DUKE IS AFTER ME. HURRY.

Waiting anxiously and trying not to panic, her heart sank when she received no reply. With trembling fingers she sent another text to Salvo and Heath.

HELP. I'M ON THE GRAVEL ROAD TO TAVERN. HIDING BEHIND LAND ROVER. DUKE AFTER ME. CAN'T RAISE JOSH. DON'T KNOW WHY. HURRY.

ON OUR WAY. CALLING POLICE.

Praying they'd arrive quickly, but not wanting to count on it, she stayed utterly still, trying to decide when she should risk climbing into the SUV. Continuously checking her watch, when three minutes passed she decided she'd waited long enough. Crawling on her hands and knees she reached the edge of the SUV, and taking a breath, she peeked around to look down the road.

"Hey, beautiful."

Duke's fingers were gripping her forearm and yanking her up before a thought could cross her mind, then spinning her around, he moved his hand across her mouth.

"You've been fun to hunt, sweetheart, but I've gotta feelin' you've called for the cavalry so we need to get the fuck outta here."

Don't panic.

Play along until an opportunity presents itself.

Anything can be a weapon.

When you fight, fight with everything in you.

Henry had taught her self-defense. Those were his edicts, and gathering her wits she realized Duke didn't have a weapon. She might be able to take him on.

"I'm gonna move my hand," he snarled, pressing his lips against her ear. "If you scream I'll fuckin' break your neck. Got it?"

As she nodded her head, she noted the position of his arm around her waist, and tried to feel where his legs were.

"We're gonna move around to the back, then I'm gonna tie you up real quick and gag you, but don't worry, we won't be goin' far."

To her great joy he began pulling her backwards. It was exactly what she needed him to do. She could use her favorite throw, but as she readied herself to kick out his legs, he unexpectedly jumped them out of the way.

"Ha. So someone's been teachin' you a few things. You think I was born yesterday? Stupid bitch. I've dealt with a lotta women just like you."

They were at the back of the Rover. She had to fight. It was now or never.

Then a miracle happened.

A blaring siren and honking horn blasted through the air.

For an instant his grip loosened.

Spinning around to face him, she grabbed both sides of his head, slammed her forehead against the bridge of his nose, thrust her knee into his groin, then shoving him on to the gravel, landed several hard kicks into his ribs with the silver-tipped toe of her boot.

WHEN JOSH AND WANDA entered the tiny cubicle, they found the paramedics had placed the victim on a stretcher and were lifting her out, but able to use her phone, Wanda placed a call to one of the young officers.

"Locate the vehicle, but only surveil until I can join you," she ordered. "If you must approach the suspect, use extreme caution. Presume armed and dangerous."

"He'll be gone," Josh remarked as she ended the call. "If he was in that clearing, he would have taken off the minute he saw the police cars."

"Not necessarily. He doesn't know we have a tracker on his truck. He might be waiting for us to leave. Wow, that went quickly," she remarked as the stretcher disappeared through the opening. "Looks like the coast is clear. Let's get out of this awful place. It's like a tomb in here."

"I need some fresh air, that's for sure," Josh replied, but as he followed her to the ladder his phone beeped, then beeped a second time, signaling an urgent text.

Wanda was about to start the climb when she felt his hand on her shoulder, and turning around, she saw fear in his eyes.

"What?"

"Let me out! Quick. I need to get out."

Jumping back, she watched him scramble up the ladder, then followed as quickly as she could, but reaching the top, he'd already rushed out the door. Hurrying after him, she saw him sprinting away from the tavern.

"Josh, wait," she yelled. "What's going on?"

"Sarge, we just got a call," the young officer exclaimed, unexpectedly appearing at her side. "Duke Palmer's here and he's got a woman named Theresa Cavalleri pinned down at her car on the gravel road."

"Holy crap. Follow me," she said urgently, breaking into a run, "and call for Mike and Dan."

But she knew there was no way she'd catch him. All she could do was pray he wasn't sprinting into danger.

Josh had always been a gifted athlete and a fierce competitor, but he'd never felt his lungs burn through his chest. His feet barely touched the ground as he ran, and as he rounded the bend and saw the Land Rover his legs carried him even faster. Wanting to kill Duke Palmer with his bare hands, he approached the SUV ready to rip him apart, but he suddenly caught sight of a man on the ground, doubled over in pain. Slowing to a stop, sure his lungs were about to explode, he dropped his hands to his knees and tried to breathe.

"Josh!"

To his great relief and Joy, Theresa was running out of the trees towards him. Straightening up and opening his arms, she fell against him.

"Thank God you're here," she panted. "I was so scared something had happened to you."

With the heat in his throat matching the heat in his chest, he closed his eyes and held her as if it was their last moment on Earth.

AN HOUR LATER THEY were back at Dream Horse Ranch telling their stories, but when Theresa complained of a headache, Josh insisted they return to the cabin. As she collapsed on the bed, he stretched out next to her, kissed her softly, then propped himself up on an elbow.

"How the heck did you get the better of that guy?"

"Henry taught me a few things, but when the car alarm suddenly started blaring he loosened his grip for a second. That was it."

"Good thing you banged the car."

"I didn't, and neither did he. It just went off."

"You must have hit the panic button on the remote somehow."

"The remote was in my bag, and I dropped it when he grabbed me. It was on the ground near the front of the Rover."

"Car alarms don't go off by themselves."

"That one did, and I'll be eternally grateful. Divine intervention," she said gratefully. "Thank you, God."

"Or Queenie," he quipped with a chuckle.

The comment had been made in jest, but when their eyes met their grins faded.

"Impossible," she whispered, feeling the goosebumps pop down her arm. "Completely impossible."

"Of course it is," he agreed, though a strange churning rolled through his gut. "Anyway, tell me, why were you in the forest when I ran up?"

"Didn't I tell you?"

"You said you were scared something had happened to me, but I don't know why."

"You didn't answer my text and I hadn't heard from you. I thought maybe Duke had a machine gun and sprayed the place with bullets."

"A machine gun?"

"I had no idea what had happened, I just knew I couldn't reach you, so I decided to creep back through the woods and approach the tavern without being seen. Then I saw you running down the road."

"Why did you go to the tavern in the first place?"

"I couldn't help myself. I had to know what was going on."

"Theresa Cavalleri, you are a very bad girl."

"But I caught the bad guy," she said with a grin, "and I don't really have a headache. I just wanted to be alone with you."

"You're changin' the subject."

"Isn't it strange how Queenie knows when we're in trouble? Heath said she was really upset."

"Theresa!"

"Okay, I admit, it probably wasn't the smartest thing I've ever done."

"Listen up. You will never knowingly walk into a situation like that again, and you will never, ever scare me like that again. And don't even think about coming back at me with any sass. Are we clear?"

"Yes, sir, but, uh, Josh, I need to ask you something. What you said when you left here this morning. Did you mean it?"

"Yes, Princess, I meant it. I meant it very much."

"Will you say it again?"

"I love you, I love everything about you, even when you pull a crazy stunt like you did today."

"Josh, I'm so happy. I love you too, so much."

"I'm still gonna tan your tail later today," he purred as he pulled her into his arms. "Hard. Real hard."

CHAPTER TWENTY-SIX

AS THE DRAMA HAD PLAYED out at the Horseshoe Tavern, Detectives Steve Yates and Jack Collins had been eating donuts and drinking coffee in their car outside Josh's house.

"He has to come back at some point," Jack muttered. "I mean, how long do you stay at a girl's house after you wake up in the morning."

"Jack, I'm married, remember?"

"Yeah, well, that's your problem. Fuck this shit," he declared, opening the door. "I'm going to have a nose around."

"Jack! Goddammit!" Steve shouted, and placing his coffee mug in the cup holder he was about to go after him, then changed his mind. "If you want to be a moron, go ahead," he muttered under his breath. "This is such a waste of time. Brady had nothing to do with any of this shit."

Picking up his half-eaten donut, he noticed a police cruiser turning the corner at the end of the block. Glancing across to Josh's house, he spied Jack peering into the side windows. He gave a quick beep on the horn to warn his partner, but Jack misinterpreted the message. Instead of ducking out of sight, Jack turned, waved, and hurried into the front yard.

"You idiot," Steve grunted under his breath, trying to signal with his hand that Jack needed to move.

But Steve's efforts were in vain. Completely oblivious, Jack walked through the gate on to the sidewalk. To make matters worse, when he spotted the approaching police car he began shifting from foot to foot, darting his eyes up and down the street as though waiting for someone. Steve cringed as he watched, and when the cruiser stopped next to his car with its window down, he lowered his and feigned a relaxed demeanor. He had a legitimate reason for being there, and he'd think of something to explain Jack's odd behavior.

"Are you Detective Yates or Detective Collins?" the officer asked.

"Detective Yates."

"Is that your partner, Detective Collins?"

"Uh-huh."

"Captain Lewis wants you both at the station right away. There's been an arrest in the Lost Time Abduction Case."

"Lost Time?"

"That's what the Captain has labeled it. Anyway, he's waiting for you."

"We'll be right there. Thanks."

"What's up?" Jack asked, trotting up to Steve as the cruiser rolled away.

"Captain Lewis wants us. He's made an arrest."

"No wonder the asshole never came home. He's in fucking jail. I told you it was him. I knew it."

"The investigation has a name now," Steve said as Jack climbed in. "The Lost Time Abduction Case."

"I like it. I wish I'd thought of it. Right. Let's go pick up that cowboy and take him back to Marionville."

ON THE DRIVE BACK TO the station, Tom had instructed Wanda to track down the location of the two detectives and send a car to deliver the news, and ask them to come to his office.

"Why don't you just call them?"

"I prefer to have a squad car give them a personal invitation."

"Don't you mean a summons?"

"No comment. Just make sure the cop behind the wheel doesn't tell them who we have in custody."

Now at his desk, with Wanda sitting in the chair by the window with her pad and pen in hand, he suppressed a grin as the door opened and the detectives walked in.

"So, great news," Jack declared as he sauntered across the room to shake Tom's hand. "Tell me the details. Where did you find the scumbag?"

"Congratulations," Steven said solemnly. "I wish I'd nailed him, but the important thing is, he's off the streets."

"That's the name of the game," Tom replied, gesturing for them to sit down. "Get the bad guys off the streets. I understand you've been staking out Josh Brady's house."

"You bet," Jack exclaimed. "I couldn't wait to get my hands on that asshole, but I guess you beat us to it."

"Take a look at this," Tom continued, tossing an evidence bag across the desk. "That was in his house."

Picking up the plastic bag, Jack studied what appeared to be a torn blouse.

"No shit. Is this from one of the victims?"

"Clothing, that's what the abductor enjoyed keeping. Like the scarf found in Josh Brady's trailer."

"Yeah, makes sense," Jack said knowingly. "I bet Brady uses them to—"

"Brady? Brady doesn't have anything to do with the abductions! Someone broke into his house last night and planted that in one of his dresser drawers."

"Huh? But that's impossible. We were outside his house."

"I know. He snuck right past you."

"But, uh, how do you know that?"

"I knew the perp would pull a stunt like that, so with Brady's permission I had someone inside his house."

"What?"

"Excuse me," Steven said. "Why didn't you make the arrest then?"

"My men followed him to see where he'd take us, but when they nabbed him, he turned out to be a local junkie thinking he'd make a quick hundred bucks. He's in lock up."

"So, Captain," Steve said, leaning forward and lowering his voice. "Who is the Lost Time abductor?"

"Abductors. Plural. Duke Palmer, the owner of The Horseshoe Tavern, and Sam Tyson, the barn manager at Tall Tree Farms. We're still tracking Tyson down, but he won't get far."

"Then I guess we'll take Palmer off your hands," Jack said with an edge to his voice. "Just tell us where to fill out the—"

"Detective Collins, this is now an ongoing statewide investigation which I have been asked to lead. I've already found two other properties in two different counties owned by his corporation and they're both undergoing extensive renovations. I suspect he had finished his hunting in this area and was about to move on. As far as charging him for suspected crimes in Marionville, you'll have to take your place in line. Thank you for your time. Someone from my station will be in touch."

"Hey!" Jack exclaimed, jumping to his feet. "Wait a second—"

"Jack, leave it," Steve said brusquely, getting to his feet and cutting him off. "Be grateful this monster has been caught."

Quickly turning and mumbling under his breath, Jack strode angrily from the room.

"Detective Yates," Tom said, before Steve could speak, "find yourself a new partner. You're a decent detective. You don't need to be saddled with him. He's in the wrong job. He should be a bouncer at a strip club. Why the look, detective?"

"That's what he did years ago before he joined the force."

"He should have stuck with it. He'd be managing the joint by now."

"Honestly, captain, I feel bad for the guy, but you're right. I'll put in for a new partner when I get back."

"Feel free to stay in touch."

"I appreciate it," Steve said gratefully, understanding Tom had just paid him a sincere compliment. "That means a lot."

Tom shook his hand, and as Steve left and closed the door behind him, Tom swiveled his chair around to face Wanda.

"Your dad will be real proud of your work on this case."

"Thank you, sir. I do have one question. How was Palmer able to fell those trees and make that clearing? That would have been a huge amount of work and it seems no-one around here knows anything about it."

"I was curious about that too. That's why I asked for the title report. The area was the original site for the tavern. Apparently the builder changed his mind. I'll bet when Duke viewed the property and discovered that hidden spot he knew right away it would be ideal for his purposes. But Wanda, this case is just beginning. He had accomplices and they need to be found. This will require a great deal of cooperation and organization. I'd like you to be the official liaison officer. Are you interested?"

"Me?"

"You've earned it."

"Oh, my gosh. Thank you, captain. Can I, uh...?"

"Hug me? Sure."

BACK AT DREAM HORSE Ranch, Carly, Heath and Andy had been discussing the arrival of a new horse. The gelding would be there on a two week trial, but with Carly in no condition to ride, Andy assumed the onus would fall on him. Heath could see Andy's concern. Being the barn's manager Andy had limited time.

"You don't have to worry," Heath declared. "I've spoken with Josh and he's agreed to give us several hours a week until Carly's back to work."

"Now that's a relief," Andy said gratefully. "Spreadin' myself that thin would've been a problem. Great news, Heath. I'll be sure and spend an hour with him and show him how things work around here. He'll be a great fit. I feel bad I didn't give him the benefit of the doubt. I won't make that mistake about someone again."

"Duke did a good job of sowin' the seeds, that's for sure."

"I'd better get back. Salvo's just cleaned out the shavin's shed and we've got a load comin' in. I need to be there to check the paperwork."

"Okay, Andy. I'll see you at dinner."

"You bet. I love Theresa's cookin'. I was thinkin' of havin' Maureen come over tomorrow night."

"Good idea. We can officially thank Josh for all he's done."

"Sounds good. I'll see you two later."

"Bye, Andy," Carly said from her spot on the couch.

"You take care now."

As Andy left, Carly smiled at her handsome husband as he left his desk and walked over to sit next to her.

"That was some morning Theresa and Josh had," she remarked. "I'm so glad neither of them were hurt by that creep."

"Yep. I think Theresa has some of your qualities."

"We get along great. I really like her, but I have a feeling she may not be around much longer. I think she'll end up living with Josh, wherever that is."

"Things will be what they'll be. Hard to say at this point, but I'm glad Josh fell into our laps. We need him and his expertise right now."

"I hate just sitting around, but it still hurts to move much."

"Broken ribs take time," he said gravely, "and you know I'm not happy about this. I told you to wait before gettin' on that horse. You knew Chuck had a buckin' issue, and I wanted Andy up there first."

"I know, and I'm sorry. I've learned my lesson, believe me."

"I'm gonna make sure about that. When those ribs are healed I'm gonna send a real strong message. You can't be so damned impetuous."

"Why are you telling me this now?" she asked, her butterflies bursting to life.

"I reckon you know the answer to that question. You wanna tell me?"

"So I can think about it?"

"Bingo. Now go get yourself some ice" he said, glancing at his watch. "It's that time."

BENT OVER JOSH'S LAP, her jeans and panties around her ankles, Theresa glanced over her shoulder with pleading eyes.

"Josh, you can stop now. My ass is stinging. I get it. I shouldn't have gone to the tavern. I'm sorry."

"You didn't just drive out there, you didn't tell anyone you were leavin', let alone where you were goin'," he exclaimed, landing another volley of hot smacks. "And just because you were able to get the better of that guy doesn't make it okay."

"Ouch, ouch, I know, I know."

"I should fetch your hairbrush." He felt her stiffen. "You've had a hairbrush blister your butt?"

"Yes, sir."

"Tell me about it."

"Henry, the biker I went out with. I, uh.."

"Go on," he ordered, landing another swat. "The truth. All of it."

"It's not complicated. I wanted to test him and I purposely did something against his wishes."

"Is that what you were doin' this mornin'? Testin' me?"

"Only partly," she admitted. "I really was going crazy."

"Thank you for tellin' me. I'm gonna give you a few more right here," he declared, touching his hand to her sit spot, "then the day after tomorrow you're comin' to my place and I'm gonna spank you again, but I'll have my bag of tricks there, and I'll introduce you to what I use to punish for testin'. What do you say?"

"Yes, sir, thank you, sir."

Lifting his leg over the back of her knees, he sent his flattened palm to the sensitive area where her thighs met her backside. Landing the slaps with gusto, she squealed and squirmed through the chastisement, then moaned as he rubbed away the sting.

"Such a bad girl," he cooed. "Don't be doin' such foolish things again."

"No, sir."

Slipping his fingers into her sex, he found her deliciously wet, and lifting his leg, he ordered her on to her knees in front of him, but as she reached for his zipper, he placed his hand over hers.

"No, that's not why you're there," he said gently. "Tell me what you're feelin'."

It took her a moment, but as she gazed up at him an unfamiliar emotion washed over her. Heat rose in her throat, and unable to stop them, tears began to trickle from her eyes. Lifting her into his lap, he held her closely, inhaling her scent and relishing the feel of her.

"Me too, Princess."

The three simple words were all he could manage. Silent minutes ticked by, and as the late afternoon wind rustled around the cabin they removed their clothes and slipped between the sheets.

"I just want to hold you," he murmured. "Just hold you and rest."

"Me too, but I must see Queenie before I go to the house and prepare dinner."

"Yes, together. We must see her together. Close your eyes. We both need a nap."

A purple sky, familiar and comforting. Pale blue cotton clouds drifted overhead, and walking through the pasture, she gazed up at the twin moons.

"There you are," Queenie declared, her white mane flowing behind her as she trotted forward. "I've been worried. We must not be separated. The end can come at any time."

"But I don't see any threat?"

"The threat will appear without warning. Where is Josephus?"

"He said he'd meet me here. I long to be crowned. I hate sleeping away from him."

"You will be crowned soon, Talini."

Turning around, her handsome prince strode across the grass towards her.

"Where have you been?"

"Teaching and healing. If I'm ever born into another life I hope to work with your tribe, Queenie. Equiannes are so much nobler than ours."

"Josephus, you must accept the inevitable. If we are so lucky we will be on Earth and you'll be human. This planet is doomed."

"Queenie, how do you know these things?" he asked skeptically. "I find it difficult to comprehend what you've predicted."

"Such knowledge is impossible to explain. I know what I know."

"Will you really lose your wings and your ability to talk?" Talini asked. "That seems so unfair."

"If I am reborn on Earth, I'm afraid so, but my other powers will be stronger. And take heart. If the worst happens those powers will see us re-united."

"But you said we probably won't recognize each other."

"I will know you. That is assured, and the attraction between you and Josephus will be strong and immediate, but it's doubtful you'll remember our lives here on Zarian."

"I will always know my Princess and my Queen," Josephus said solemnly. "In my heart, I will always know."

"And I will too," Talini exclaimed. "I will always love Josephus, and you will always be my Queen. Will you rule as you do here on Zarian?"

"No, but I will rule. It is in me. I will rule and love those worthy, and there are none as worthy as the two of you."

"What is that light?" Talini asked, her eyes darting to the sky.

"It's time," the mare said, unable to hide the tremble in her voice. "Stay close. It's time."

"It's time. Theresa, wake up. It's time."

"No, no, I don't want it to be."

"You're dreaming. Wake up," Josh said, grabbing her flailing arms. "Wake up!"

Eyes wide, Theresa stared up at him, then threw her arms around his neck.

"We lived on another planet, Queenie was our Queen. You were my Prince and I was your Princess."

"What a lovely fairytale. Kind of like we are now."

"You don't understand."

"I understand you need to get yourself together and up to the house."

"It's fading. I don't want it to fade."

"The dream? Dream's always fade."

"It's gone. Phooey. My butt hurts."

"Good. Now get it out of this bed."

"Josh?"

"Yeah, Princess."

"I loved Henry, but not the way I love you. I feel as if I've been with you forever. Like I've found a home."

"I feel that too," he said softly. "Who knows? Maybe we were together once, and we've found each other again."

"I'm going to believe that."

"I think I will too. You, me, and Queenie," he murmured, sliding his fingers into her hair. "And I'm sealin' it with a kiss."

EPILOGUE
Three Days Later

UNDER CLEVER QUESTIONING by Tom Lewis, Derrick Palmer boasted endlessly about his heinous crimes and how he'd thwarted the police. After his many years on the force Tom thought he'd seen and heard just about everything, but when he asked why they'd found no forensic evidence, Derrick's answer astounded him.

"A wet suit."

"Did it have some kind of opening in the front? You must have used one hell of a condom, or did you wash your victims when you were done with them?" Tom pressed, still confounded. The wet suit would have been extremely effective, but even using a regular condom there should have been some speck of DNA.

"I didn't have sex with them," Derrick replied, his face contorting into an ugly scowl. "That's gross. Women are disgusting, but I enjoy playing with their naked bodies while they sleep. I'd get my jollies watching them suffer in the pit, then when I'd get back."

"Very considerate of you to leave their wedding rings and phones. What was that about, Duke?"

"Mmmm," he purred, the frown dissolving as a faraway look crossed his eyes. "I'd watch them stumble around and search for their phones. Then they'd have to try to find a spot with a signal. Hah. The panic in their voices—loved that."

"And the rings?"

"The rings were too fiddly. Too hard to get them off with my gloves. I didn't give a shit."

"Why did you keep Claudia Harris for so long?"

"Tits. She had great tits. Too much fun for just one night, and I needed to let her loose up near Springdale while Brady was there."

"What about Sam and the others you do this with. Do they wear wetsuits too?"

"Watching. Helping. That's it. If they touched one of my harem I'd cut their fuckin' balls off and they knew it."

"You're a sick, twisted bastard, you know that?"

"When I hear people like you say shit like that, it makes me think you're just fuckin' jealous."

"Why don't you think about this?" Tom growled, leaning across the table. "Justice tends to move slowly, but I'm going to make sure this case moves as fast as it possibly can, and when the time comes I will personally drive you to prison. I'll take you through the doors, and I'll make sure everything is arranged so you'll receive the kind of welcome you deserve."

JOSH HAD RECEIVED AN invitation from the owners of Tall Tree Farms, John and Terry Coleman, to join them for coffee. The request was unique, and he assumed they needed to speak with him about Sam. The recent news of the barn manager's death on the mountain road, and his involvement in the Lost Time Abduction case, would have deeply shaken the elderly couple.

On his way he'd had an errand to run, and he smiled at the package sitting next to him on the passenger seat. He'd woken with the idea in his head, and compelled to act, he'd driven to the only store he thought would have it in stock. When he'd walked in the very item he'd envisioned was on display. He'd never bought a gift like it, but to his amazement the color and size were exactly right, extinguishing any lingering doubts.

As he drove past the barn and up to the house, Ben and Jerry greeted him with excited leaps and kisses. They'd seen little of him during the past two days. Though he'd put all lessons on hold, he planned to resume the schedule over the coming weekend, but without a barn manager he wasn't sure exactly how things would work. Climbing from his car and walking on to the porch, the front door opened as he approached.

"Ben and Jerry are our doorbell," Terry said with a welcoming smile. "How are you, Josh? Please come in. You've become quite the town hero."

"I'm fine, but how are you two coping? I'm sure learning about Sam must have been a terrible shock."

"It was, it really was. We're still coming to grips with it. Come into the living room. John's in there by the fire. His arthritis has been acting up."

"Hello, John. Sorry about all the trouble."

"Terrible business," he said gravely. "Terrible. Have a seat."

"Thank you."

"Do you take cream?" Terry asked as she poured the coffee.

"Yes, please."

"I hope you don't mind, but I'll get straight to the point," John said gravely. "It's pressing on me."

"I completely understand."

"Terry and I love our horse farm, but we've decided it's become too much for us."

"And the weather," she said. "Our bones can't take another snowy winter, and the worry about the yearly storms are too much."

"We're moving to Florida to be with our children and grandkids," John continued, "but we don't want to sell to just anyone. Would you be interested? You know this property's quirks so you won't be in for any surprises, and we'll tell you all about this house. We built it, you know."

"My goodness. I wasn't expecting this, and I'm truly honored that you've offered it to me."

"If we can arrange a private sale and not have to pay a realtor's commission, we could both save money. I have a lawyer who can draw up the sales contract."

Josh's immediate reaction was a resounding yes, but sensing the couple needed to talk, he held back and let them. An hour, two cups of coffee and three slices of home-made cranberry cake later, they shook hands on the deal. Theresa wasn't due at his house until after dinner, but unable to wait, he called her and told her he was on his way to see her at Dream Horse Ranch, and to wait for him in her cabin.

"What happened?" she asked as he walked in. "You look like you just won a million dollars."

"First, I have a present for you," he declared, handing her the box. "Sorry, I didn't have time to wrap it."

"Wrapping is overrated," she said with a grin. "What did I do to deserve this?"

"Just bein' who you are. A vision of it came to me and I had to buy it for you," he answered, feeling oddly awkward. "I hope you like it."

As she lifted the lid and pushed aside the tissue paper, she stared in astonished delight at the chocolate-brown suede jacket with sheepskin lining.

"The color matches your hair."

"Josh. I can't believe it. Honestly, I can't. I absolutely love it. I love it more than you can know. Thank you so much."

"You're welcome, Princess," he said with a wide grin, slightly embarrassed, but touched by her enthusiastic response. "I'm glad you like it."

"You didn't hear me. I love it," she said excitely, pulling it on and spinning around. "It fits me perfectly. Now tell me the news, though I can't think of anything that can match this."

"I think it might. I just bought Tall Tree Farms."

"You're kidding?"

"Nope.'

"That's fantastic," she exclaimed, throwing her arms around his neck. "I'm thrilled for you."

"I want to change the name though. I need to completely expunge Sam's association. What do you think of Queenie's Horse Ranch. Where Horses Reign?"

"I just felt a funny tingle," she murmured, tilting her head to the side. "I think it's perfect. Yes. Let's go and tell her."

As they stepped outside and looked towards her paddock, they found her staring up at the cabin.

"How cute is that? Whoa. What's she doing?"

The mare had suddenly broken into a jig, then exploding into a series of bucks and spins, she began galloping around the paddock and whinnying loudly.

"She knows," Theresa declared. "She knows and she's celebrating. Josh? Why are you looking at me like that?"

"I know something too," he said, placing his hands on either side of her head. "This was all meant to be. You, me and Queenie. I love you. You're my Princess. I want to carry you over the palace threshold when I take ownership."

"Yes, please," she managed, as the happy tears sprang from her eyes. "The funny thing is, I set out to catch a cowboy, but I have this feeling Queenie lassoed both of us."

THE END

Dear Reader:

Thank you for buying this book. If you have a moment I would greatly appreciate your review. I constantly strive to bring you interesting and enjoyable content and your feedback is valued. Feel free to contact me at any time. I love to hear from readers. My email is: MagCarpenter@yahoo.com, and here are my social media links should you care to check them out.

Maggie

http://www.MaggieCarpenter.com
https://www.facebook.com/MaggieCarpenterWriter
https://twitter.com/magcarpenter2
Subscribe to Maggie's Newsletter @ MaggieCarpenter.com[1]

---

1. *http://MaggieCarpenter.com*

BOOKS BY MAGGIE CARPENTER

ROUGH COWBOY
COWBOY
His Ranch. His Rules. His Secrets)
TO KISS A COWBOY.
TO CATCH A COWBOY.
TO CON A COWBOY.
TO TRUST A COWBOY:

SEXY SCIFI - PARANORMAL

ROUGH ALPHA
TRAINED BY THE ALIEN:
WARLOCK :
THE ALIEN'S RULES:

BDSM CONTEMPORARY ROMANCE

www.ingramcontent.com/pod-product-compliance
Lightning Source LLC
Chambersburg PA
CBHW021030130626
46552CB00005B/1767